GUNFIGHT AT HILTON'S CROSSING

Drifter Chuck Mellors is wondering where his next dollar will come from when he receives an enticing proposition from an unpleasant man. Inveigled into assisting in a robbery which goes terribly wrong, he soon becomes a fugitive from the law. Seeking justice not only for himself, but also for the widow and child who are suffering as a consequence of the crime, Chuck Mellors embarks upon a long journey through the Indian Territories to Texas. Here, in the little town of Hilton's Crossing, matters reach a shocking and deadly resolution.

BILL CARTWRIGHT

---◆---

GUNFIGHT AT HILTON'S CROSSING

Complete and Unabridged

LINFORD
Leicester

First published in Great Britain in 2017 by
Robert Hale
an imprint of The Crowood Press
Wiltshire

First Linford Edition
published 2020
by arrangement with
The Crowood Press
Wiltshire

A catalogue record for this book is available
from the British Library.

ISBN 978–1–4448–4407–8

Published by
F. A. Thorpe (Publishing)
Anstey, Leicestershire

Set by Words & Graphics Ltd.
Anstey, Leicestershire
Printed and bound in Great Britain by
T. J. International Ltd., Padstow, Cornwall

This book is printed on acid-free paper

1

Chuck Mellors's troubles began in earnest on the day that he agreed to help two men retrieve the deeds to their farm, out of which they had been cheated, or so they claimed, in a crooked poker game. The recession which gripped the United States in that year of grace, 1871, had been going on now since nigh-on the end of the war and showed no present signs of abating or diminishing in the slightest degree. Labouring men like Mellors were a positive drag on the market and it had been better than a month since he'd had any work.

That summer's evening, he was eking out a glass of porter in the Last Post saloon. If he didn't find some way of making money soon, then he didn't know what was to become of him. His only possessions — bar the clothes he stood up in — were the mare, currently in a field back of the livery stable down the road aways, a beat-up old musket and the Navy Colt at his hip. If things got any worse, he might be obliged to dispose of one or the other of these; if, that is, he wanted to eat. It was while in this despondent frame of mind that a sharp-faced man, whose physiognomy put Chuck Mellors in mind of an especially crafty and unpleasant weasel, sidled up to him and said quietly, 'Hey, tiny, you want to earn yourself fifty dollars?'

It should perhaps be mentioned at this point that Mellors was exceedingly tall and broad and it was not at all uncommon for men who supposed themselves witty and amusing to address him by epithets such as 'tiny' or 'shorty.'

'You say what?' said Mellors. 'Fifty dollars? I should just about say that I do. What's afoot? Meaning what have I to do to earn the money?'

'Most nothin' at all,' replied the ill-favoured individual who had made the offer. 'Just look as though you might break somebody's neck if they don't do

2

as they're told, is all.'

'This ain't involving some strong-arm stuff? I'm not one for beatin' up on folks, less'n I got good cause.'

'Lord, no,' said the man, 'nothing of the kind. Here, finish your drink now and take a turn up the street with me. I'll set the case out for you.'

As the fellow explained to Chuck Mellors, he and his cousin had been lured into a poker game the night before, which was not all that it had seemed. The two men had been led on, allowed to win a fair bit and then finally got caught up in a fierce round of betting. So unbeatable had his hand been, that the weasely-looking man, whose name was apparently Flint, had foolishly put into the kitty the deeds to a farm which he and his cousin had just purchased. His four knaves had been beaten by queens and all their money was gone and the farm into the bargain.

'We found out later as the men who were running that game are bent as they come. We'd been rooked like a pair

3

of damned rubes.'

'So where do I fit in?' asked Mellors in some perplexity. 'What do you actually want me to *do*?'

'Like I said, you just got to stand around looking like you might hand out a hiding to this fellow, if'n he don't let us have back those property deeds.'

As is sometimes the case with very large men, Chuck Mellors's great physical size was not matched by the strength of his intellect and he saw nothing untoward or strange about the story that Flint told him. A shrewder man might have asked a number of pertinent questions before becoming embroiled in the affair, but apart from all else, Mellors desperately needed that fifty dollars; it represented an amount of money that he might have had to work hard for two or three weeks to earn, in the usual way of things. Assuming that there was work available that is, which at that moment, there was not.

'So where is this man who's got your farm?'

'We got to meet up with my cousin Red. He's a skinny little thing like me,' said Flint, 'which is why we need a big man like you to help us get what's due us.'

So far, none of this struck Chuck Mellors as being in any way out of the ordinary. This man and his cousin had been cheated and were simply aiming to regain the property which was rightfully theirs. A sharper and less trusting man might have asked himself why the men had been carrying the deeds to a farm about with them like that and whatever would have possessed them to hazard such documents in a game of cards with strangers. None of this occurred to Mellors, though. He was in general one for taking things at face value and believing what he was told. It would be unkind to describe the man as being simple, but there were certainly more quick-witted and agile-minded men in this world than Chuck Mellors.

Flint's cousin Red turned out to be a scrawny, mean-looking man of about thirty, whose flaming ginger locks explained at once the origin of his nickname.

'You'll help us?' he asked Mellors, when once they had been introduced. 'Good man. Here's your money now. Just be ready to lend a hand if need be, that's all.'

Once again, it might have occurred to some men to ask how, if these two men had lost all their money at a game of cards, Red still had five ten dollar bills, ready to hand. Mellors, though, just tucked the money gratefully into his pocket without thinking any further about it and said, 'Well then, when do we go after these fellows?'

'The man who has our deeds is staying over the way, right on the edge of town,' said Flint. 'No reason we shouldn't call on him right this minute, if you're willing?'

'Suits me well enough.'

'Let's go, then.'

The twilight was darkening, turning the sky purple. The deepening shadows caused the shabby little Kansas town of Perseverance to look almost pretty. The darkness hid the peeling paint and crumbling masonry of a town which was long past its prime.

The boarding house was set right where the town ended and the prairie began. This establishment catered for those men passing through Perseverance who were not content to settle down with their blanket-roll in a barn or out in some field, just beyond the town's limits. The rooming house was for those who actually required a bed for the night, in other words.

'Ain't we a-goin' to knock on the door?' asked Chuck Mellors, when Flint gripped his arm and guided him to a shadowy space between the last two stores on Main Street.

'Not nohow,' said Flint, 'we can see the door from hereabouts. That'll about do. We can brace the fellow when he comes out.'

Slow on the uptake as he sometimes was, even Mellors noticed that whereas before, the talk had been of a group of men running a rigged poker game, it now looked to have narrowed down to one individual person. He remarked upon this seeming anomaly, only to have the man known as Red growl, 'You want to hand me back that money? No? Then quit askin' all these questions and just do as you're bid.'

The three of them stood there silently for upwards of a quarter of an hour. Then the front door opened, spilling an elongated rectangle of soft yellow light across the street.

'That's him,' said Flint. 'You get a-ready now, big man. Here's where we take him.'

The man who left the boarding house didn't, at least to Mellors's eyes, look much like a cardsharp. Indeed, had he not known better, he would have had him pegged for a farmer. For all that he was wearing his Sunday meeting clothes, he definitely had the air of a man who worked the land. Mellors couldn't have said just why he had that impression, other than that he'd grown up on a farm himself and recognized the type.

One thing he did mark was that this man was burly and had the confident air of a fellow who knew how to take care of himself. Those two skinny types who had enlisted his aid would have been hard pressed to tackle this man alone.

As the man moved towards Main Street, with the evident intention of heading into the centre of town, the three men stepped out of the shadows and confronted him. He stopped dead in his tracks and said, 'Hey fellows, what's to do?'

'Don't you give me that,' said Flint roughly. 'You know what we want.'

Watching the man's face, Chuck Mellors saw a dawning realization, which lead him to believe that this fellow knew precisely what was going on. He said to the man, 'Come now, why don't you just hand over what's theirs and then there won't be any unpleasantness.'

'Unpleasantness? That supposed to be a threat? And who the hell are you, anyways?'

'Just hand it over,' said Red, 'and then nobody'll get hurt.'

'The hell I will!' said the man, who then commenced shouting at the top of his voice, 'Hey! There's a man here being robbed! Help!'

Flint muttered an oath and then said to Chuck Mellors, 'Catch a hold of him there! Just grab him.'

Without really thinking about what was going on, Mellors threw his arms round the bellowing man and enveloped him in a bear hug. This didn't stop the fellow hollering so Red made a swift movement, which was followed by a ripping sound, as though somebody had torn a piece of fabric. The yelling ceased immediately and was transformed into a cry of pain, which faded after a few seconds into a gurgling groan. Then the fellow went limp in Mellors's arms.

Even before the man had stopped making a noise, Flint and Red were going methodically through his pockets, until Flint gave a cry of triumph and held up a sheaf of documents, saying,

'That's it. Let's make tracks.'

Although the street was deserted at this end, the shouting had prompted people to throw open their windows to see what was going on. Flint and Red had simply sprinted off, without even saying farewell to Mellors, who now found himself holding what felt like an unresisting dead weight. As soon as he let go, the man fell at once to the sidewalk. Mellors bent over to see what ailed the fellow, gripping his lapels and shaking him a little, only to recoil in horror and disgust when he found that his hands were slick with blood. At which point, he did what he had been apt to do since the end of the war, whenever things got too much for him; he simply dug up and ran. It was not that he was a coward. Anybody who had fought alongside Chuck Mellors in the late War Between the States would have scorned such a suggestion. Rather, all the fighting and din of battle over the course of those four grim years had somehow effected a mischief in the man's brains, whereby he easily became overwhelmed and had to make off quickly to be by his own self and get his thoughts in order. Such was the case now.

Mellors's horse was in a corral at back of the livery stable and his saddle and pack were in the barn there. He'd paid in advance for two nights so he did not need to worry about any formalities, but just tacked up the mare and made off into the night. By the time anybody started any serious investigations into the death of the man he had been holding, he'd be some miles away. Not that he had reasoned out the case to that extent; merely that he knew fine well that he could not bide there in that place another minute.

As he rode along the track leading into the hills, Chuck Mellors thought about what had happened in the last hour. It had all occurred so quickly that he felt a little giddy. One minute, drinking peaceably in the saloon and now on the run for, well, he supposed that the fellow was dead, so that would make it murder. The enormity of the thing had yet to sink in.

The track he was riding upon was used only by hunters as a rule; it didn't really lead anywhere in particular, other than to some scrubby pine forests. Mellors had marked the winding trail when he hit town yesterday as somewhere leading south that might be worth looking at, if he had to live rough for a bit. He was capable of catching enough game and fish for his own dietary requirements, and he had been growing that low on cash money over the last week or two, that he was beginning to think that he might do worse at this time of year than go up into the mountains and live off the land for a time. After this latest incident, the attractions of this course of action had now become all but irresistible.

After leaving town at a gallop, Mellors thought it wise to slow down a mite, now that he was clear of danger, at least for the time being. He didn't want his mount to break a leg in the dark. It was about midnight when he stopped. Maybe somebody could follow his trail up here, but the chances were that if anyone was planning to pursue him, then they would wait until it was light.

In any event, nobody came after Chuck Mellors the next day. He moved further from the town at day-break and found a secluded little hollow in the foothills of the mountains; a place where he could set up camp and use as a base for hunting. There was a little stream nearby, where he was able to fill his canteen and take the mare to drink, then and when. He was quite nicely set up there and although he could have done with some bread to accompany the roasted squirrel that he brought down and fish that he tickled out of a stream, he could survive well enough like this for a week or so. It was a monotonous diet, enlivened only by a few berries that were in season, but there were worse things in life than not having sufficient variety in your vittles.

The next four days passed uneventfully, Mellors being unwilling to venture onto frequented roads until he was sure that the fuss would have died down about the business with that fellow dying like that. Because he had really not known what was planned and was therefore innocent of any wrongdoing, Chuck Mellors didn't treat the whole matter as being all that serious. Sure, he knew that men got their necks stretched for murder, but when all was said and done, he'd done nothing, nothing at all.

From time to time, other men would be glimpsed in the distance. Mellors assumed that these were hunters or travellers. Anyway, they did not trouble him or, as far as he was aware, even notice his presence up here on the edge of the mountains. On the morning of the fifth day of his little expedition, he went off shortly after dawn to see if he could catch some bigger game. There's not an awful lot of meat on a jackrabbit and Mellors was beginning to think that if he could catch himself a pronghorn, then that would keep him going for a while. His efforts were not crowned with success and he returned to his camp site empty-handed. It was not until he was over the crest of the ring of rocks which protected him from view in that hollow, that he saw that he was not alone. Two men were waiting for him and they both had rifles aimed right at him.

'What's to do, boys?' called Mellors to the men, who were thirty yards off. 'You want somethin'?'

'Well, first off is where we want you to drop that rifle o' your'n,' said one of the men. 'Just you let it fall now, you hear what I tell you?'

'Surely.' He released his grip on the rifle and let it clatter to the rocky ground.

'Now you walk on, real slow, towards us.'

As he strolled forward, Mellors said, 'What's this all about? You fellows aimin' for to rob me?'

16

The one who had not yet spoken laughed out loud at this and then said, 'Us rob you? You're funny, you know that?'

'If you ain't robbin' me, then what's the game?'

'The game,' said the man who had ordered him to drop his rifle, 'is that we are taking you back to Perseverance to hang for murder. There's a price on your head, mister. You thought you could come skedaddle up into these hills and folk'd forget about you?'

'You're taking me in for the reward? You ain't law or nothin'?'

'Not a bit of it. This here's what you might call a strictly personal enterprise.'

Chuck Mellors was now standing right in front of the two men and looked at them with disgust in his face. 'Why, you're no better than bounty hunters! Law's one thing, men like you is somethin' else again.'

'Shut your mouth,' directed the man who had told Mellors that he was funny. 'Just shut your mouth and come closer. I want to tie your hands. First off though, I'm going to take that pistol from your holster.' He fitted the words to the actions and reached forward to disarm the man in front of him.

It was the first time that these two individuals had ever tried something of this sort. They were not professional bounty hunters, but had heard of the reward being offered for the apprehension of the three men who had robbed and killed the farmer a few days ago. One of them had come up into the hills to hunt and seen a very tall and broad man who looked to be living wild up there and had then enlisted the aid of his friend to see if they couldn't collect the $100 reward being offered.

If the two fellows who were now attempting to set up as bounty hunters had had any sort of experience of this kind of work, then they would not have allowed their quarry to approach so close to them. But they had Mellors pegged for a slow-witted, slow-moving oaf, who would be too daunted by their levelled rifles to think of resisting.

For a man of such size and bulk, Chuck Mellors was capable of an astonishingly rapid turn of speed when the circumstances required it. He did nothing obvious and crude such as grabbing at the rifles which were pointing in his direction. Instead, he stepped swiftly between the levelled guns and, stretching out his arms to their fullest extent, swept his two hands together. The two men who were covering him were standing barely three feet apart and Mellors was easily able to catch each one of them around the side of the head. He brought their two heads crashing together with a bang which echoed around the little hollow in which they were standing. Then, while they were stunned and barely conscious of what was going on around them, he deprived them of their rifles, reached down and took their pistols too and then stepped right back, so that he would be out of their reach when they came to.

The look of dismay on the men's faces when they realized the sudden reversal of fortune which had befallen them was comic. Mellors didn't waste any time gloating though, merely observing, 'I don't reckon you boys are cut out for this line of work.'

'What're you going to do?' asked one of the men fearfully. For reply, Chuck Mellors picked up one of their rifles, gripped the barrel in one hand and the stock in the other and then, exerting his full strength, bent the barrel and splintered the wooden stock.

'God almighty,' mumbled the other man, 'I never saw the like. You going to kill us?'

'No, but I'm a-goin' to take your horses with me aways before setting them loose,' said Chuck Mellors. 'And I'm 'fraid I'll be takin' your guns, too. A man can't run too many chances and I don't trust you boys not to come after me.'

Although he was leaving them up there, weaponless and afoot, neither of the men voiced any complaint. They knew that they were lucky to escape with their lives.

2

When he was a child, Chuck Mellors had a reputation among his schoolfellows as a tale-bearer and sneak. Indeed, his nickname in the neighbourhood, at least among other children, was 'Tattletale' Mellors. This was unfair, because it was less the case that young Chuck was anxious to get others into trouble for their misdeeds, than that he had exceedingly firm notions of right and wrong. If he saw injustice, then he could not rest. Even those who called him 'Tattletale' were forced to concede that Chuck Mellors would as readily challenge a teacher or other adult about what he saw as unfairness, as he would somebody his own age. None of this was undertaken to his own advantage, but was more in the nature of an impartial quest for a world where everybody got his just deserts.

All of which goes some way towards

explaining the brooding sense of wrong which possessed Mellors as he rode south, following the confrontation with the two amateur bounty hunters. He had offered to help out a couple of fellows who told him that they had been cheated and appeared to have a genuine grievance. They had paid him for his help and all he had done was grab hold of a person who he took to be a cardsharp. How could he possibly have been expected to know that those men were up to no good?

It was plain that remaining in the location of the town where all this had lately happened was not the smart move for Mellors so he had to dig up and move on. But he was not only fleeing from the fear of death, whether at the hands of vigilantes, bounty hunters or due process of law. For Mellors, a wrong had been done, both to him and most likely the man who had been killed while he, Chuck Mellors, was holding him. He had done the right thing in running from the scene, of that he was sure, because in the immediate aftermath of such crimes, folk can be mighty hasty about stringing up whoever they judge to be answerable for the crime. But now that he was clear of the danger of hanging, Mellors began to consider how to put things right. The most obvious way of doing this, as far as he could gauge, would be to lay his hands on the men who had inveigled him into the crime and hand them over to the law. He did not consider this course of action in the light of any reward and nor did he stop to think that he might himself end up in the same gaol cell if he wasn't careful. It was simply what was right.

With fifty dollars in his pocket, Chuck Mellors was now able to stay in a rooming house, which is what he did several days after leaving the mountains, when he was on the very edge of the Indian Nations. The town of Walker's Landing lay on the banks of the Arkansas River and was the last civilized spot before the territories began. It was far enough from Perseverance for Mellors to hope that word of the murder in which he had unwittingly been involved had not yet spread. In this he was mistaken, as he discovered after booking a bed for the night, while he wandered down to the saloon to slake his thirst. There were only two other men in the bar, neither of whom seemed inclined to converse, so Mellors took his drink over to a table, where there lay a copy of the newspaper for this part of the state. It was, according to the bold, Gothic heading, *The South Kansas Plain Dealer, incorporating the Walker's Landing Agricultural Gazette and Intelligencer.*

It must be said that Chuck Mellors was not a great reader; in fact, he'd not picked up a book since his schooling had finished fifteen years previously. Nevertheless, he could generally make out most of the words in a newspaper of this sort and even when he couldn't quite grasp an unfamiliar word, he could, as a rule, make sense of it by the context. Laboriously, and with a good deal of licking of his lips and hard concentration, he worked through the paper. There was little of interest though, until he reached the sections dealing with the sale of agricultural machinery and so forth. There, on the opposite page was an article whose headline contained the name of the town in which he had last stayed. He read, VICIOUS MURDER BY GANG IN PERSEVER-ANCE: LOCAL FARMER SLAIN. After reading this, his heart sank, but he knew that he had to discover the worst so he carried on to see what else he might learn. The article read as follows:

Consternation and alarm were the order of the day in the quiet town of Perseverance, when a brutal murder took place there on the 18th Inst. Those of us who are familiar with Perseverance, know it as a pleasant, if somewhat backward little place. More than once, it has been com-pared to the village of Sleepy Hollow, as depicted by the famous writer MR WASHINGTON IRVING. On

Monday 17th July, MR RICHARD CARSTAIRS, a local farmer, had come to town in order to affect the sale of his property. He told a friend in town that he thought that a watch had been set upon his movements and had been made uneasy on that account.

Having received payment for his land, in the form of $3,000 worth of bearer-bonds, Mr CARSTAIRS returned to his lodging house. That evening, he was attacked in the street and relieved of the bonds, which are not at the time of going to press, recovered. There are said to be three assailants. One is described as 'a mountain of a man', being exceedingly tall and with a breadth and girth to match. Another has vivid red hair, while the third is described as being a 'ferrety-looking individual'. The sheriff's office in Topeka has posted a reward for information leading to the apprehension of any of these suspects.

Regular readers of this newspaper will be aware that we have inveighed for years against the issuing of bearer-bonds, which may be cashed in anywhere and are as good as cash money. They are an open invitation to robbery. It is thought that the miscreants in the present case are 'playing it carefully' and are most likely to be heading south through the territory of the Five Civilized Tribes. Selling the bonds would perhaps invite fewer questions in Texas or Mexico than it would anywhere in Kansas.

A melancholy addendum to this story is that the wife and child of Mr CARSTAIRS are likely to be thrown off the farm by the new owner. Having parted with $3,000 to purchase the spread, he told your correspondent that he feels no obligation towards Mr CARSTAIRS's widow and her child. This unfortunate woman and her family are accordingly likely to be indigent and without a roof over their heads in a very short time.

* * *

Having read through every word of the piece, Chuck Mellors put down the paper, gulped down his drink and left the saloon.

Reading that newspaper article had brought forth two differing emotions in the breast of Chuck Mellors. On the one hand, it seemed likely, now he was well clear of Perseverance, that he was in no danger. He wasn't the only tall and well built man in Kansas and nobody would have any particular reason to connect him with the robbery. Then again though, there was the fact that he had been inveigled unwittingly into participating in a robbery and had his neck put in hazard. More than this, the crime had left a widow and her child at risk of being turned out of their home and left to fend for themselves. Neither of those things were right.

As he walked up and down the boardwalk, Mellors thought about what else the newspaper had said. Those men, Flint and Red, were most likely heading through the territories, if what was written was true. Like as not, if they had gone down that way, they would stay there for a spell, laying low. Well then, what was to hinder him from going there himself to find them and call them to account? He had a crow to pluck with them on his own account for treating him like a fool and getting him mixed up in a hanging matter. Not only that, but they had the money that rightly belonged to the widow of that poor fellow they'd stabbed. Surely, that should be returned to the rightful owner, which was to say Mrs Carstairs?

It was getting dark now and Mellors did not feel minded to start a long journey as night was falling. But there was no reason why he shouldn't set off for the Indian Nations the very next day. He had most of that fifty dollars left, which would buy a little food and in any case, his luck hadn't been anything to write home about here in Kansas. Maybe things would change once he was across the line and in the territories.

After his first night spent in a bed for some good while, Mellors felt thoroughly invigorated the next morning and sprang up, ready to tackle the world. Before collecting his horse, he stopped at the store to buy a few provisions for the journey. The clerk was happy to chat about this and that. 'Fine weather we been having, wouldn't you say?'

'I reckon so,' said Mellors. 'I'm heading south today. You think it's apt to remain dry?'

'Don't see why not. Where you going? Texas, I'm guessing.'

'Why, yes. How'd you guess that?'

'Lot o' folk moving around just lately. Huntin' for work and suchlike. There surely ain't much doing hereabouts. You plannin' on passing through the territories?'

'I should say so.'

'Well,' said the clerk, 'you look like a

man as can take care of his self. It can get rough down in those parts, you know what I'm saying?'

'You mean Indians?' hazarded Mellors.

'Them as well. It's more all the outlaw types hiding out down there. Place is a regular pest-hole.'

This sounded quite promising to Chuck Mellors and tied in with what that newspaper had hinted at. He said, 'That ain't just stories as the newspapers put about?'

'Not a bit of it. 'Cause this here is the last town 'fore you get to the county line, we see all sorts and conditions o' men going that way. Half of 'em are men you wouldn't care to break bread with, not if you was starving!'

Once he'd paid for all the bits of provisions he was taking with him, Mellors thought it worth taking a slight risk. He said, 'You seen any such comin' through here lately?'

'Any such what?'

'Men as you think might be on the run.'

After having been so easy and friendly, the man behind the counter froze up at the direct question, saying, 'Couldn't say. None o' my business, when all's said and done. I'll be wishin' you a very good day, mister.'

It was only after he'd left the store that it struck Chuck Mellors that for the first time in his life, he had perhaps been mistaken for a bounty hunter. The thought made him chuckle.

No visible border marked the boundary where the state of Kansas ended and the Indian Nations began. Chuck Mellors had been riding for most of the day before he saw another white man. He had passed the occasional Indian and once an entire family, but these people had ignored him. It was late afternoon when he came upon an old man ambling along upon a donkey, whom he overtook a few hours before the sun went down. As he rode level with the man, he said, 'Good evening to you, sir.'

The old man looked round at him

sharply, saying, 'If you're planning to rob me, I can save you the trouble. I've nothing worth stealing.'

Horrified that anyone should place such a construction on a simple, neighbourly greeting, Mellors replied, 'I ain't a-plannin' to rob you, sir, nor nothing like. I was just being friendly. Why, I'll ride on past you right this second if it'll ease your mind any.'

The man shot him an appraising glance and said in a quiet voice, 'Don't you mind me, son. I lived among thieves and bandits that long, I have grown out of the habit of trusting my fellow men. It is a sin. I'd be glad of your company for a little.'

The two of them rode side by side in companionable silence for a while, until Mellors asked, 'I'm right in guessin' that this is the territories we're in now?'

'Right enough. You're among those whose spiritual needs I tend to, the good Lord preserve you.'

'You ain't a missioner? You live in these parts?'

'I do, my son. And a heavy cross it is to bear, too. Are you seeking information? As to being a missioner, not exactly. But that don't signify.'

'Have you come across two men moving south through here?' asked Mellors. 'One with bright red hair and the other a face like a weasel? Meaning sharp and cunning with teeth like a rat?'

'Why do you ask? Are you looking for them so that you can do them a good turn or an ill one?' When there came no reply, the old man said, 'What are you about? Lawman? Bounty hunter?'

It was the second time that day that Chuck Mellors had been suspected of pursuing this most loathsome of careers and he laughed out loud. 'Lordy, but you are the second man today to suspicion that. I ain't no bounty hunter. Nothing like. I'm lookin' for those boys on a personal matter. I been wronged.'

'Wronged? Ah, you're on the vengeance trail, is that the way of it? Tell me about it.'

Mellors hesitated, plainly wondering

how wise it was to reveal that he was wanted for murder.

The old man made an impatient sound. 'Tush, man. I'm not going to concern myself in your affairs. Anything you tell me will stay safe with me. It's between you, me and the Almighty. Why are you seeking those men?'

Slowly and haltingly, Chuck Mellors reasoned out the case to the man, who listened carefully without interrupting. At the end of the story, the old man summed up the matter succinctly, by saying, 'So you're on a vendetta, hunting for these men to do them harm, on account of the injury they caused you? That won't do. Did you never hear the Scripture, 'Vengeance is mine, saith the Lord. I will repay'?'

'Heard it, right enough,' said Mellors stolidly, 'but I never set a store by it. There's another reason I want to find them fellows, 'part from my own grudge.' He talked about the family of the late Richard Carstairs, who faced homelessness and penury due to the loss of the family breadwinner and his being robbed of the money paid for the farm. Mellors finished by remarking, 'While you're a-quotin' the good book to me, seems to me as I recollect something about the Lord caring specially for the widow and the child. Or maybe I misremembered that part?'

The old fellow looked at Mellors as though he might have been mistaken in his estimation of him and said, 'Ah, you're sharper than you look at first sight. Don't crowd me though, for it's a thing I can't endure.'

They continued for a time, neither of the men speaking, until at length the man said, 'You might find word of most anybody passing through these parts at a little cantina, lies maybe seven or eight miles further along the road here. The man who owns it is called Joe Abbot and he's not as bad as some men in these here parts.'

'You coming along that way as well?'

'No, I turn off to the east in another half mile. You want to get along there, you just leave me to my own devices.'

'I don't like to leave a man o' your age unprotected — ' began Mellors doubtfully, before the other interrupted him with great irritation.

'Old man, nothing. I've lived and worked in these parts for over a decade. I'll do well enough. Go along with you and if you get back this money for the family, then I hope you'll think twice before spilling blood in the doing of it.'

'So long then, sir.'

'Goodbye, son, and God bless you.'

Mellors felt strangely heartened by the encounter with the old man. He had the distinct impression that the fellow had known something of the men he was tracking and had mentioned this Joe Abbot's place with a view to setting his feet on the right trail. He proceeded at a trot, leaving the other man to carry on along the road at barely a walking pace.

*　　*　　*

Scattered throughout the territories at this time were various white men who contrived to make a living from trading with the Indians or catering to the needs of white men. Some such entrepreneurs, and Joe Abbot was one of the breed, did their best to combine both activities. Now technically, at least according to the many solemn and binding covenants which had been signed between the government in Washington and the chiefs of the five civilized tribes whose land this was in theory, white men were forbidden to live or settle in the Indian Nations. However, such prohibitions had always been honoured more in the breach than in the observance.

Abbot's place was part trading post and part eating house and saloon combined. He supplied the Chickasaw with cheap tinware and gaudy luxury items such as mirrors and strings of shiny beads. These, he traded for pelts, furs and anything else that he could sell on for a profit. That was one half of his establishment. The other half was to be found around the back of his stone house, where Joe Abbot had constructed something like a lean-to against the back wall of the house. Here, he dispensed cooked food and hard liquor to passing white men. 'Abbot's Place', as it was universally known among those who frequented that part of the Indian nations, was where men stopped off for food, drink, company, news and information. It wasn't large; there was scarcely room for more than a dozen men to sit crammed side by side on the rough wooden benches. Its virtue lay in the fact that here was somewhere that those on the edge of the law could meet up and speak freely with each other. Almost all the clientele of Abbot's place were up to some species of villainy; be it moon-shining, gun-running or just something as innocuous as the illegal buying and selling of gold.

From the outside, as he approached it, Joe Abbot's place looked so unprepossessing that Chuck Mellors was not sure if it was where the old man had been directing him. There was no sign up over the door to suggest that this was anything other than a private residence. Mellors reined in his horse and sat for a while, watching the stout and imposing building, wondering if he should simply ride on and knock at the door. There was a barn nearby and a corral, which contained a number of horses. He rode a little closer and then went off the road, so that he could get a better view of the property from the rear. Once he had done so, he saw that there was what could pass for an eating place.

The way he saw it, Mellors didn't have a great many options open to him at that moment. He was in unfamiliar territory and looking for two perfect strangers. There'd be no point in wandering aimlessly round the Indian Nations, hoping to bump into a man with bright red hair. Besides which, he'd formed the idea that the fellow on the donkey had been hinting that the two men for whom he was searching might have been through or past this place. He checked his pistol, spinning the cylinder and then making sure that there were caps on all of the nipples. When he was satisfied that the Colt was in good order, he thought about how he was going to frame his enquiries. Then Mellors started the mare walking towards the house.

3

Joe Abbot's place was somewhere that men on the scout could relax and be themselves. At a saloon in a normal, civilized town, you never knew who might be listening to your conversation or whether somebody would go sneaking off to the sheriff after overhearing about some action which sounded as though it might be illegal. It even happened sometimes that the man standing next to you at the bar might turn out to be a sheriff, deputy or marshal who was off duty. At the little cantinas one came across in the territories, this was very unlikely to be the case. Many of the men knew each other, at least by sight, and a stranger who looked like he might be the law would stick out a mile and be the object of suspicion.

As he neared the lean-to, Chuck Mellors could hear the shouting and laughter of rough men at their ease. He was puzzled when all conversation died away as he entered the little room and walked towards the planks laid over the tops of two barrels which served as a bar in Abbot's place.

'Any chance of a bite to eat?' asked Mellors, in a friendly voice. 'I'm fairly starved.'

'Got pork and beans,' said Joe Abbot.

'Gee, I ain't too fond o' pork. What else you got?'

Abbot shrugged indifferently. 'That's it. Pork and beans. You want it or not?'

While he was talking to the man behind the planks, Mellors was aware that conversation had started up again, although in a low and subdued hum rather than the raucous and good natured racket there had been when he walked through the door.

'You want a drink with that?' asked Abbot.

'What you got?'

'Whiskey.'

'What else?'

Joe Abbot looked irritated. He said,

'Listen, pilgrim, this here isn't one o' them fancy hotels like you get out East, with shining silverware and white damask tablecloths. You want a greater variety, happen you come to the wrong joint.'

'I guess whiskey will do just fine,' said Mellors hastily, not wanting to create any ill feeling. After all, he was hoping to pump this fellow for information shortly and it wouldn't do to put him out of countenance before he'd even asked a single question. 'You look like you do a good trade here,' he remarked conversationally, as Abbot was spooning beans into a grimy bowl. 'Must be a regular little goldmine, spot like this.'

Joe Abbot said nothing.

'Fact is,' said Mellors, deciding that a direct and manly approach might work better, 'I'm looking for a couple o' men who might have passed through here.'

'That a fact?' said Abbot, in a voice which did not invite further questions. 'I don't hardly notice the faces of any of my customers here. Sorry I can't help you.'

'Well,' persisted Mellors in an amiable and engaging way, 'you might recall one of the fellows, on account of he had the brightest red hair you ever did set eyes upon in all your born days. Hard to miss, I'd say.'

'Would you?'

'Why, yes. You seen anybody fittin' that description?'

While he was chatting, in what he thought was an innocuous way, to the man behind the bar, Chuck Mellors failed to notice two men get up from one of the nearby tables and walk over towards him. They took up positions right behind him and one of them then proceeded to jab him hard in the back with his fingers, which were rigid and bony. He turned to face them, saying, 'Hey, you fellows, don't be doing that now, 'cause I don't take to being prodded and such-like.'

Even the quiet conversation had now ceased again entirely and the attention of every man in the room was focused upon the drama which they assumed

46

was about to unfold up at the bar. Abbot, sensing the mood, had abandoned his post and retreated to the house. His policy in the case of fighting or shooting was clear-cut and sensible. He neither wished to be shot nor to witness anybody else being shot, stabbed, beaten or otherwise assaulted. In the event that anybody came asking questions at some later date, as had once or twice chanced, he was able to state with perfect honesty that he hadn't seen a damned thing, on account of he'd popped out to answer a call of nature.

'Don't like being prodded, hey?' asked one of the men. 'You shoulda thought 'bout that 'fore you started askin' a heap of questions.'

Like many exceptionally big men, Chuck Mellors was familiar with the kind of fellow who makes a point of picking a fight with the largest and tallest man in a bar. Although he wasn't himself one for fighting and brawling, Mellors was no coward and did not allow others to take liberties with him. He said, 'Listen, the two of you. I'm not wanting a lot of nonsense, fighting and such.'

'What you want an' what you're going to get is two different things,' said the man. 'We don't take to strangers marchin' in here and cross-questionin' folk like we was in a courtroom.'

Even now, things could have passed off without any violence, if the other man, who had not yet spoken, hadn't spat on Chuck Mellors's boots. Mellors looked at the man and said quietly, 'You are one filthy devil, you know that?'

It was obvious that these boys were intent on a fight so Mellors didn't see any point in delaying matters further. His right hand shot out like the piston of a steam engine, catching the man who had spat over his boots clean on the jaw. A fraction of a second later, Mellors drove his foot down as hard as he could on the instep of the other fellow and before he had a chance to react, grabbed his belt with one hand and his shirt-front with the other and swung him up, throwing him against his friend, who was just rising from the floor. This had the effect of sending one of the tables over and causing the men who had been sitting there, to leap up angrily, swearing and cursing.

After having created all this disorder, Chuck Mellors just stood there, easy as could be, seeing what would come next. He had a gun at his hip, but he doubted that this would be a killing matter. The men he had dealt with got gingerly to their feet, wondering what to do next. Before they had a chance to collect their scattered wits, Mellors said loudly, 'Listen here, you all. I've not come here to cause anybody problems. Those boys just now was lookin' for a fight and they found it. That ain't my fault. I'm a-searchin' for two men who wronged me. They tricked me into a robbery and now it's life and death, for I'm wanted for murder. More than that, the man they killed and robbed, his widow and little 'un are beggared and have nowhere to lay their heads. I aim to get back their money. Now all I ask is if anybody seen two men, one with very red hair?'

There was a dead silence and it looked like he was not going to acquire so much as a scrap of information here. Leaving the food and drink he'd ordered, Mellors turned on his heel and left the room. As he strode out, he more than half expected somebody to launch themselves at his back, although this didn't happen.

Outside, it was twilight and Mellors stood by his horse, wondering what to do next. Then a man came out of the cantina, stood a few feet away, and proceeded to make water. Mellors turned away, disgusted, but the fellow said softly, 'Those men you're after, they was here not forty-eight hours since.'

In a similarly quiet voice, Mellors said, 'Any notion where they're to be found now?'

'There's a fellow who runs a cathouse maybe twenty miles south of here. Calls his self Seward. That's where those boys are headed, for a bet. Sorry for your misfortune.'

'Thanks.'

Then the man spoke again, only this time his voice was harsh and unfriendly. He said loudly, 'Yeah, you get along out o' here, you sneaking cow's son. We don't want no informers nor any such round these parts!'

Looking round in surprise to see what might account for this sudden change in tone, Mellors saw that another man had come out of the cantina, evidently with the same physical intention as the first. Presumably, the man who had tipped him the wink didn't want to be thought of as helping him. Mellors said mildly, 'I'm on my way.'

It would be night soon and Mellors thought that he should probably find somewhere to sleep. He knew little about the territories and honestly didn't know if he was apt to wake up with his throat cut if a bunch of Indians came upon him slumbering in their land. It would, at any rate, do no harm to exercise a certain amount of caution. He was toying with the idea of riding up into the woods which rose along one side of the track, when he heard hoof beats behind him. Judging from the rhythm, the riders of what he judged to be two horses were in an uncommon hurry to get somewhere.

It was a hundred to one against the riders coming up behind him having any interest in him or even noticing him, if he moved off the road, but at the same time, Chuck Mellors thought it would do no harm at all to be prepared. He took the pistol from its holster, cocked it and then held it, not openly as though he was looking to use it, but half concealed in the mane of his horse. If there was the slightest chance of fighting, he didn't aim to be stopping an arrow or bullet in his back so Mellors turned his mount and began walking it at a steady pace back towards the oncoming horsemen.

It did not really come as a great shock when, from the darkening gloom, emerged the two men with whom he'd had the set-to at the cantina. As soon as he saw who it was, Mellors reined in his horse and waited patiently. They were seemingly a little taken aback to find the man they were after facing them, ready and waiting. They too, came to a halt.

'Well, boys,' called Chuck Mellors cheerfully, 'what will you have?'

'You shamed us back there,' said one of them, 'everybody started laughing at as after you left.'

'Can't say as I blame 'em. You started something you couldn't finish.'

'You bastard. Will you give us satisfaction?'

'I got pressing business. More important than this foolishness. I'm sorry if you and your partner looked like fools, but maybe another time you'll think twice 'fore you start jabbin' a man in the back and spitting at him. Stuff like that's bound to end badly. But if you'll have a duel, then sure.'

While he was speaking, Mellors unobtrusively began to raise his pistol. The one who had spat on his boots said, 'You think you're pretty damned smart, don't you?'

'Not specially,' said Mellors. 'Smarter than you, maybe.' He levelled his gun at the man who'd spoken and fired at once. Despite all this talk about giving them satisfaction, it looked as though neither man had been prepared for action, because as his ball hit one of the men in the chest, the horse of the other man reared up in terror, nearly throwing the rider. By the time this fellow had got his mount under control again, Mellors had him covered. There was no way in the world that he would have been able to draw and fire, before the man in front of him gunned him down.

The man he'd shot had fallen from his horse and lay still. Mellors remarked phlegmatically, 'Soon as you asked for satisfaction, that's when you shoulda shot me. All that talking, you just took your eye off what you was doin'. Talkin's one thing, fightin's something else again.' He said this as unemotionally as if he had been giving advice about fishing or playing ball. The man watched him fearfully, wondering if he too was about to die.

'I guess you're anxious to know if'n I'm a-goin' to shoot you, too,' said Mellors, like he might have been discussing the weather. 'Well, I don't reckon as I am. But I will if you put me to it. You want more shooting?'

'No. No, I should say that I didn't.'

'Good man. You just turn around now and ride back the way you came. You carry on ridin' down that track 'til I can't hear you any more. You stop or turn back, I'll kill you.'

'What about Walt?'

'What about *what*?'

'Walt. He's my partner that you done killed. I can't just leave him lying in the road. It ain't fitting.'

'You can come back for him after I've gone. I ain't going to trouble his body.'

The man stared at Mellors for a space and then said, 'You are one cold-hearted bastard, you know that?'

'Seems to me that if the pair of you

hadn't come troublin' me, none of this woulda happened. You went looking for trouble and you found it.'

The man said nothing more, but turned his horse around and trotted off into the darkness. Mellors listened carefully for any sign that the rider was stopping or riding in a circle and coming back again, or any of the sort of tricks that men sometimes play under such circumstances, but all he heard was the fading sound of the hoof beats as the man rode back up the track. When there was silence, he rode off in the way that he had been going before he was interrupted. This time, he knew for sure that he would have to conceal himself well, because that man whose friend he had killed would certainly be wanting to deliver retribution if the opportunity presented itself.

For another mile, Chuck Mellors carried on south and then veered off the road towards the woods. When he reached them, he dismounted and led the mare carefully along a narrow and ill-defined path. As he walked along, he thought about what had just occurred and ran over it all in his mind, just to assure himself that he had not behaved dishonourably. Those men had demanded satisfaction and he'd told them they could have it. When all was said and done, that was when they should have been on their guard and ready to fight. It was hardly his fault if they'd followed up this direct challenge with a lot of point-less talk! If you issued an invitation to a duel, then you really needed to be ready for action at once. Chuck Mellors didn't see that he had anything to reproach himself with and when he found a secluded and cosy spot to rest, he drifted off to sleep with no more bad conscience than if he'd been a new-born baby.

* * *

Some thirty years before Chuck Mel-lors was wandering south through the Indian Nations, a man called Michael Seward had had a strange ambition. It was 1840 and the railway mania was gripping the nation. There was talk of a line running south from Kansas to Texas, and Seward figured that there would be a fortune to be made for the enterprising man who built the first hotel along the likely route of this line. Surely, if there was a commercial hotel in the middle of the wild country, then that would be sufficient reason for the railroad line to establish a way-halt within easy reach of the place. This at least was how Seward reasoned out the case.

There were those who said that Michael Seward wasn't quite right in the head and that the idea of building a commercial hotel in the middle of nowhere, in Indian country to boot, was a crazy one. Still and all, Seward had the money and he hired an architect, and paid for men to help him in his dream. The completed building was of more modest proportions than most hotels, having only a dozen rooms, but the thing was built. It surprised nobody that the business was a resounding failure and few even raised their eyebrows when Seward shot himself a year and a half later. It only went to confirm what some folk had thought all along, that the man was plumb off his head. Travellers privately called the place 'Seward's Folly' and with the death of the owner, most thought that the establishment would soon fall into ruin.

And there the matter might have ended, had Seward's nephew in Boston not inherited the little hotel and decided that he rather fancied the notion of setting up home away from the big city. Jim Seward was twenty-five years of age at the time. He moved into the strange and useless hotel and lived there. Travellers did pass by the building, but they were less interested in comfortable beds, than they were in women and drink. So it was that little by little, young Seward found himself running firstly a saloon, of sorts, and pretty soon a cathouse, too. From the beginning, it was a very democratic and egalitarian establishment, with a few outcast Indian girls and one or two white women. Somehow, word got around and Jim Seward found that both Indian men living nearby and white men passing through had a desire for simple and uncomplicated sexual liaisons, for which they were prepared to pay.

This was not exactly the career that the young man had envisaged when he left Boston, but there were worse ways to make a living. Nobody was forced into doing anything and the girls were grateful for a base from which to work. He took a percentage of their earnings and supplied drinks as well and the little one-time hotel flourished.

Of course, there were slack periods when there were no customers and nothing coming in and this led to Seward's Hotel, as people still referred to it, branching out a little, into the real hotel business. From time to time, some man would turn up at the hotel, wanting somewhere to live for a week or a month.

Most of these men were outlaws, needing a place to hole up, but Jim Seward didn't ask any questions about that, it was just what he assumed. Anyway, these characters wanted rooms for more than just somewhere to spend an hour with a whore. That was fine, because there were never more than one or two such people at a time and it didn't interfere with the running of the hotel in general as a brothel. This then was the establishment to which Chuck Mellors was headed in the high summer of 1871.

4

Two days before Chuck Mellors fetched up at Abbot's place, a couple of riders had reined in outside Seward's Hotel. Both were scrawny and undersized; one had a mop of flaming red hair. This man said to his companion, 'What say? We stay here for a couple o' days, maybe three? I sure could do with a rest.'

Jake Flint, the man to whom he addressed this question, nodded and said, 'Can't see any reason why not. I could do with a screw, too. I'll warrant you could as well.'

'You got that right!'

Jake Flint and 'Red' Tom Halliday really were cousins; practically the only truthful thing that they had told Chuck Mellors. They lived their lives from day to day, mostly making ends meet by cheating at play and small robberies, although they sometimes joined with others and went after bigger prey, such as stages or trains. Over the last month, they had had what they perceived to be a run of luck, which culminated in the murder of Richard Carstairs and the theft from him of every cent he possessed.

Robbing Carstairs had been a consequence of the merest chance. Flint had been standing on the boardwalk looking at some pipes in the store window, when two men came out of a doorway by the side of him. He found later that this door led to a staircase, which was the way up to Perseverance's only attorney's office. The two men who came out of that door stood for a moment, shaking hands and exchanging a few final words. One of them said, 'You take good care of those bonds, sir. You know anybody can cash them.'

'Feel safer that way. Know what I'm about,' said the other man.

'Even so, that's a lot of money to have in your pocket. You take a care now, Mr Carstairs.'

That brief snatch of conversation was all that Jake Flint caught, but it was more than enough to set him on the trail. When one of the men turned and went back through the doorway, Flint glanced round and saw the discreet, brass plate which announced that this was the registered office of David Sterne, Attorney at Law. At once, this told Flint that if some client had just left with some bonds, that it would be no trifling sum. Generally, people in those parts only used attorneys if they were proving a will, selling their house and so on. This was very promising so he at once set off after the other man, the one he assumed to be the attorney's customer.

Flint had a name now and it was from catching stray crumbs like that, that he and his cousin had in the past made large sums of money. The man whose name was Carstairs went straight from leaving his attorney into the Last Post saloon. Unobtrusively, Jake Flint followed him in and stood nearby at the bar, as the barkeep joshed with Carstairs about being a rich man now. Although the fellow serving the drinks didn't apparently know about these bonds that Carstairs had in his pocket, it seemed to be common knowledge that he had recently sold up and was moving East with his wife and daughter.

Where money was involved, Flint had a pretty sharp memory and he went over what he had heard the attorney say. He had mentioned bonds and said, 'Anybody can cash them.' Putting it altogether, it would appear that this man Carstairs had sold a farm and was carrying the proceeds of that sale around with him this minute in the form of bearer-bonds, which were utterly untraceable. It was perfect. Mind, if he and Red could get hold of them, they'd be best to take them to Texas, maybe even Mexico to dispose of them. That was fine, they needed to get away from Kansas for a while anyway.

After just the one drink, Carstairs bid

farewell to the barkeep and intimated that he would be back in two hours, when he was meeting a friend at the Last Post. Flint trailed him to the boarding house he was staying at and then went in search of Red Halliday.

The whole thing had gone like a dream and now here the two of them were, ready to bide their time for a little while, before carrying on south and crossing the border.

After spending the better part of thirty years running a brothel and drinking hole, Jim Seward bore little resemblance to the eager and enthusiastic young fellow who had arrived from Boston all those years ago. He greeted the two newcomers amicably enough, asking, 'What'll it be, boys? Girls, whiskey or a room for a while? Or all three?'

'You got a room we could use for a few days?'

'Sure,' said Seward. 'Quiet right now. Girls are at a loose end, too, some of 'em. They'll be rarin' to go, if you know what I mean.'

So it was that Red Halliday and his cousin moved into a room at the remote little hotel in the middle of the territories and, as far as they were aware, not a living soul knew of their whereabouts. The pair of them felt as secure and unworried as anybody in their line of work was ever apt to feel.

*   *   *

Chuck Mellors had the happy knack of being able to get a good night's sleep most anywhere. He awoke the day after killing the fellow from the little cantina feeling as fresh and lively as if he'd been slumbering in a feather bed. He was not a callous or violent man by nature and yet it must be remarked that it was not until he had been up and about for over an hour that he even recollected shooting the man dead the day before. This was because in the first place, he had never seen much point in fretting over things that were finished and done with, and secondly, because he believed that he had acted with perfect correctness over the dispute which had led to the fellow's death. Those two men had been determined to start a fist fight with him and then when that didn't work out for them, they had challenged him to a more deadly combat, only to come off worse again.

It looked to be a bright, sunny day, which always lifted Mellors's spirits. He'd no food with him so he contented himself with a few swigs of cold water from his canteen. He'd have to see if he could shoot something later, that was all.

Once he was in the saddle and heading south, Mellors felt a little better about life. The day was fine, he was still alive and free and, with a little luck, he should soon be able to right the dreadful wrong that had been done to both him and the widow and child of the man who'd been killed in front of him. He wasn't an especially religious or superstitious man, but Chuck Mellors knew fine well that the blood of the late Richard Carstairs was crying out for justice. However unwittingly, he had had a hand in that innocent man's death so it fell to him to right the wrong that now threatened to make beggars of the wife and child left penniless.

The track that he was following, too vague and indistinct to be called a road, meandered south, leading deeper into the Indian Territories. Mellors had heard recently where the Indians were supposed to be currently at peace, but even so he felt a mite uneasy. One man with a single pistol was not apt to be any match for a whole band of redskins, should they be in a warlike mood. Still, there it was. There was little enough to be done about it. Every so often, he encountered lone riders and even one or two men on foot, either going in the same direction as him or coming towards him. All were Indians and none acknowledged his presence, despite Mellors crying, 'Good morning to you!' cheerily to each of them.

It was nearing noon before anything

of note happened, by which time Mellors was beginning to feel a little giddy with hunger. The road was passing through a patch of scrubby woodland, when away over to his right, Mellors heard what sounded to him like a child's voice, crying out in distress. He had something of a soft spot for children, not that he ever had many dealings with them, but when he did, he always enjoyed their company. It would have sat ill with him to cock a deaf ear to a child calling for help, particularly in such a remote and uncivilized area such as this. He accordingly reined in the mare, dismounted and made his way towards the voice, which was now whimpering in real fear or pain.

Although he'd no reason to apprehend any kind of danger, Chuck Mellors had never found that a little caution went amiss so he eased the Navy Colt from the holster at his hip, cocking it with his thumb as he did so. Then he slipped forward a little further, until he found himself on the edge of a little glade, where a truly shocking sight presented itself to him. A white man with his pants down around his ankles was trying to force himself upon a young Indian girl who to Mellors's eyes looked to be no more than fourteen or fifteen years of age. The girl was fighting like a wildcat and yelling in terror, while the man tried to keep hold of both her wrists at once while also raising her dress.

The would-be rapist had his back to Mellors, but the girl caught sight of him and began screaming even louder in some unknown language, doubtless appealing for his help. Realizing that she was calling to somebody behind him, her assailant whirled round and, catching sight of Mellors, said, 'You better walk on by, you hear what I tell you? This ain't none o' your affair!'

'I ain't so sure 'bout that,' replied Chuck Mellors mildly, 'it surely looks to me like something's going on here as I don't care for.'

The man glanced to a nearby tree,

beside which some of his gear was stowed. Mellors followed the man's gaze and then continued in a pleasant way, as though conversing with an old acquaintance, saying, 'I reckon you're wondering if you can jump over to that rifle o' your'n yonder and shoot me down before I can get a good shot at you. Well, you are surely welcome to try.'

'Well, what will you have?' said the man, evidently deciding that it would be little short of suicide to dive for his weapon while Mellors was drawing down on him with his pistol. Then he had a sudden inspiration and suggested in a friendly voice, 'Say, what say we share the squaw, turn and turn about?'

So disgusting was this last suggestion, that for a moment Chuck Mellors was tempted to shoot down the wretch on the spot. Only the fact that he might end up killing the girl as well stopped him giving serious consideration to such a course of action. Instead, he limited himself to telling the fellow,

'Move away from that young lady and take off your pants entirely.'

The man looked at him stupidly. 'What d'you mean, take off my pants? You tryin' to shame me?'

'You already done that for your own self, carryin' on so,' said Mellors. 'I tell you now, my patience is all wore away. You don't do as I bid you, I'm like to shoot you down like the mangy cur you are.'

There was a quiet finality in his voice which had a sobering effect on the fellow who had been troubling the Indian girl. With no more ado, he moved away from her and sat on the ground to remove his pants. He had to take off his boots to do so and when he'd finished, he presented a ridiculous figure; standing there barefoot and naked from the waist down. 'What now?' he asked, his voice a little husky with apprehension.

'You walk away.' The man reached for his boots and Mellors stopped him with a gesture of his pistol, saying, 'No, you won't need your boots. Just get off now, as you are. You're getting off light. There's some as would have killed you for what you were tryin' to do.'

Without any more debate, the half-naked man walked off through the trees. He wasn't carrying a gun-belt and as far as Mellors could see, the rifle leaning against a nearby tree had been his only weapon. The girl watched as Mellors gathered up the rifle, pack, pants and boots and made a little heap of them in the middle of the clearing. Then he went over to the pony tethered nearby and untacked it, placing the saddle atop of the other stuff. As an after-thought, he took the rifle and swung it several times against a tree, until the barrel was bent a little out of shape. Then he slung it back on the heap and went in search of some twigs and branches. Unhurriedly, Mellors built a fire around and beneath the man's belongings, which he kindled with a Lucifer. When it was blazing merrily, he turned to the watching girl and said, 'I don't know if'n you speak

English or no, but you best come along aways with me, 'til we're clear of here.'

The girl made no reply, nor gave the least indication that she understood what had been said, but followed Mellors back to where he had left his horse. As they threaded their way between the trees, he wondered if he had been too hard on the man whose property he had so peremptorily destroyed. It was a fearful thing to deprive a man in such wild country as this of the means to defend himself. Then he glanced at the girl behind him and his heart hardened. He had, after all, left the fellow his mount and that was more than he deserved. He might cut a bizarre spectacle, riding back to civilization bareback and without his pants and boots, but at least Mellors had left him with his life, which was more than some might have done.

When they reached the mare, Mellors said to the girl, 'Don't suppose you speak English at all?' When she did not reply, but instead stared blankly at him, he continued, 'I guess there's no point in askin' where your folks live. I can't leave you here, with that skunk still in the area, so all I can think of is that you better come along with me for a spell.' Mellors added under his breath, 'Not that it ain't a damned nuisance, mind.'

When the girl still said nothing, he indicated that she should mount his horse. She hopped nimbly enough up into the saddle, with such swift proficiency that it looked to Mellors as though she was quite at home on horseback. He said, 'I hope you ain't fixin' for to steal my horse, little lady? That'd be the hell of a thing after me rescuin' you an' all.'

The two of them made their way along the little track, Mellors holding the bridle and the girl seemingly content to sit astride the horse and see how things developed. After a short time, they found the trees petering out and the man and his companion emerged on to a scrubby and barren plain, with nothing to break the monotony as far as the eye could see.

'Least we're not apt to be ambushed,

that's one mercy,' said Mellors, half to himself. 'Thing is though, I'm losing time here and at this rate, I'll never catch up with those boys. How am I ever to be rid of this child is more'n I can fathom.'

There was still no present prospect of eating, which was beginning to be a serious problem for Mellors. He was better able than many to make do on short commons but he still needed something in his belly. This particular problem solved itself in the neatest way imaginable. Here and there across the landscape were scattered trees, most of them stunted and looking as though they were struggling to survive. Ahead of them though was a mighty oak, which looked to be stone dead. As they drew close, it was possible to see that the tree was blackened and scorched, as though it had caught fire some time in the past. Mellors guessed that it had been struck by lightning. While he was musing on this, he noticed a twitching movement about twenty yards away and saw that several groundhogs were squatting at ease and watching him without showing any particular fear. He halted and drew his pistol. Softly, he reassured the girl by saying, 'Don't be affeared, honey. I'm a goin' to try and provide us with vittles.'

The crash of the pistol shot rolled across the plain like thunder, but wrought the desired effect by bringing down one of the little critters. The Indian girl didn't even flinch at the sound of gunfire. On a hunch, Mellors waited quietly to see what would chance and, as he had hoped, when the echoes died down, another hog poked its nose from out of its burrow and two minutes later, had hopped completely into view. This one too fell prey to a .36 ball.

To his surprise, the girl jumped down at once from the horse and scooted over to pick up the dead creatures, evincing no disgust at the blood with which they were besmeared. She said something in her own language, gesturing imperiously to Mellors. He knew instinctively what she was after, and took out the hunting knife which rested in its sheath at the rear of the saddle, handing it to the Indian. Then he walked over to the old tree and was pleased to discover that there was plenty of dry and partially burned wood lying at the base of it. In next to no time, he had kindled a cheery blaze. While he was doing so, the girl set to gutting the groundhogs, expertly preparing them for broiling.

Once they had eaten, Mellors felt a deal more satisfied with life. He asked the girl again if she had any folks hereabouts and then tried haltingly to explain that he would not be able to travel along with her indefinitely.

'Fact is, I'm hunting for two bad men,' he said. 'Very bad men, and I got to catch up with 'em, see. Which I can't with you tagging along.'

On hearing the words 'bad men', the Indian looked sharply at Mellors and through a mouthful of meat, repeated his words. 'Bad men. You look bad men?'

'Oh, so you do understand something, hey? You know 'bout bad men, is that it?'

The track that they had been moving along ran dead south. The girl jumped to her feet and pointed to the right of the direction that the track went, away over to the west. She said clearly and distinctly, 'Bad men! Bad men! I take you.'

'You want to take me to some bad men, is that the way of it? Or are you telling me that you know where bad men go?'

They had almost finished eating now and Mellors was eager to be on his way. He had privately decided that he would escort the girl for the rest of that day and then try and disengage himself from her. After all, this was her territory and as long as he was sure that she was safe from the man who had been molesting her, he didn't see that he was called upon to do much more.

It was plain that the girl was determined to direct Mellors in a direction different from that which he was set on. To begin with, she declined to mount the horse and instead grasped the bridle and began to lead the mare west, instead of south. At first, this was irritating, but as he tried to wrest control of the beast from her, the girl became most insistent, saying loudly, 'Bad men. I take you!' She would by no means relinquish her hold on the bridle and in the end, it seemed easier to allow her to have her way. She seemingly knew something that Mellors didn't and since he had only the vaguest idea where those two rascals were to be found, he figured in the end that she might know something more about the business than he did himself.

'All right,' he said, after attempting in vain to wrestle the bridle from the girl's grasp and start leading the mare south again, 'I guess you win. You're a-goin' to take me to where there are bad men, is that it?'

'Bad men. I take you!' she replied and so he suffered himself to be led west and hoped that the Indian knew what she was about.

5

After a pleasant and energetic night of sexual congress with an athletic young squaw, Red Halliday had finally fallen asleep an hour or two before dawn. He was jolted into wakefulness at about ten that morning, by somebody pouring a trickle of cold water on his face. Opening his eyes, Halliday saw an unfamiliar face leaning over him. Not being accustomed to allowing folk to take liberties with him, Red Halliday sprung into action at once, driving the other man from him by lashing out with his foot. He followed up this manoeuvre by leaping from the bed and grappling with the fellow, knocking him to the floor and then sitting on the man's chest. It was only then that he recognized the intruder and said, 'Jackson, you bastard. One of these fine days, fooling around like that's goin' to get you killed, you know that?'

'If you say so,' replied the man, with a chuckle. 'Let me up, you oaf. You're crushing me to death.'

Once he was up, Tom Jackson walked over to the room's single easy chair and threw himself down upon it, leaving Halliday to perch on the edge of the bed.

'What brings you to these parts?' Halliday asked.

'Might ask you the self-same thing,' replied the other, 'but I ain't a-goin' to. That'd be looking a gift horse in the mouth, as the sayin' goes. Fact is, Red, you're the answer to a man's prayers.'

At this, Red Halliday laughed out loud. 'I been called a heap o' things in my time, some of them none too pleasant, but this here's the first time anybody called me the answer to their prayer.'

'Still and all, that's how the case stands, my boy. Tell me now, how're you and that cousin o' yours fixed for cash money? Seward told me that you and him fetched up here together.'

Halliday eyed the other man dubiously. 'We's doin' well enough,' he said cautiously. 'What you asking 'bout our affairs for like this?'

'Lordy, but you are a suspicious devil. Anybody ever tell you that? Here am I, bringing you the chance of a lifetime and all you do is stare at me like I've come here to rob you.' Jackson made as if to rise from the chair, saying, 'Happen as I should take my proposition elsewheres.'

'Ah, sit down,' said Halliday, 'you're too touchy for your own good. Just lay down your hand and tell how matters stand.'

Tom Jackson, who had not had the slightest intention of getting up and leaving, made an expression as if to hint that he was mighty put out. Even so, he consented to set out the scheme which he calculated would bring a reward of $4,000 each to him, Halliday and his cousin Jake. He said, 'You know the Katy Flyer runs through the territories?'

'You mean the train?' asked Halliday.

'No, you lunkhead, I mean the hot air balloon. Of course the train.'

'What of it?'

'It runs up from Texas, little place called Denison. Goes up towards Parsons and towns north of there. Get to the end of the track, it turns around again and heads back to Texas.'

'I could find out all this from a railroad timetable,' growled Red Halliday. 'Whyn't you come to the point, you wordy bastard?'

'Well then, here 'tis. There's a fellow in Parsons runs a bunch o' stores. Jewellery and such. He's pulling out o' Kansas, can't find the profit there, see. What it is, he's bundlin' all the stock of those stores up and entrusting the whole caboodle to the secure van on the Katy. Something like twelve thousands' worth of earbobs and gewgaws, nothing you could trace in a hundred years.'

'And your plan's for us to take down the Katy Flyer and lift this cargo?'

'You got that right, boy. You in or you

out? You best make your mind up pretty damned soon, 'cause if'n you don't want in, there's others as will.'

For a space, Halliday said nothing, concentrating on making his face look as impassive as could be, while his mind was racing furiously. He knew Tom Jackson well enough, had even worked with him on odd occasions. Knocking over a railroad train, although not something entirely new in Halliday's experience, made him pause and weigh up the odds. Then, he thought, surely the three of them would be able to stop a train and then somehow persuade those in charge of the van to part with the property they were engaged to protect? Combined with what he and Jake already possessed in those bearer-bonds, why, it would mean that they wouldn't have to work for the foreseeable future! Hell, they might even be able to put some of the cash into somewhere permanent, maybe a little farm or something.

At last, Halliday shrugged ungraciously and said, 'It sounds like a pail of hogwash to me, but if there's aught in it, then me and Jake might lend a hand. I ain't promisin' nothing, mind. We needs must see what my cousin thinks of the idea 'fore we can get any forrader.'

'Sure thing,' said Jackson, his voice betraying a mite too much over-eagerness. 'I ain't askin' you to buy a cat in a sack, nor nothin' like.'

Jackson's response told Red Halliday almost all that he needed to know. Here was a man who was plumb desperate to find partners for a criminal enterprise. Presumably, this was because he was working against the clock. No doubt this famous consignment of gold would be travelling through the territories very soon and Jackson didn't have time to find anybody else to aid him in robbing the train.

Halliday said casually, 'Mind, me and Jake, we got a heap of things doin' right now. I can't see us being free for something like this for a week or two at least.' Just as he had expected, Jackson cavilled at hearing this.

'The Katy Flyer leaves Parsons day after tomorrow. We got forty-eight hours to fix it all up. I tell you now, it's cuttin' it damned fine. You ain't interested, just tell me now.'

'Hell, seeing as how it's you askin', Tom. Yeah, I reckon me and Jake's in.'

All the time that Red Halliday and Tom Jackson were talking over their plans, they gave no more thought to the young Chickasaw woman lying in the bed than they would have a cat or dog. Like most of those who visited Seward's 'hotel', they treated the Indians they encountered there with complete contempt; hardly viewing them as being human beings at all. This could on occasion prove a mistake, because some of the women working as prostitutes had long memories and were always on the scout for ways of supplementing the meagre living they scraped by at Seward's place.

★　★　★

The day after Tom Jackson showed up at Seward's Folly, Chuck Mellors mounted the crest of a low hill and thought that his eyes must be deceiving him. There, shimmering in the distance and looking as though it were almost floating above the dusty plain like a mirage, was a little commercial hotel of the sort that one might come across in almost any town served by a railroad. True, it looked a little run down and dilapidated, but it was indisputably an ordinary hotel, although what it was doing out here in the middle of nowhere was a regular conundrum.

When the little Indian girl saw the hotel, she clapped her hands in delight and turned to Mellors, saying, 'Bad man place.'

'Place where we're apt to find bad men, is it? How d'you say we should approach? Am I in hazard if I just walk up and rap on the front door?'

Now although he had no reason to think that the girl understood his words, Mellors had observed that she seemed to be adept at interpreting his tone of voice and gestures. She took his arm and pointed towards a stand of trees about a quarter mile from where they were standing. Then she began to lead his horse in that direction. He said, 'You want me to stay out o' sight 'til you know how the land lies, is that the game?'

Once they reached the copse, the girl indicated by dumb show that Mellors should stay there, quiet and out of sight, until she had been to the strange building and spoken to somebody there. He couldn't see any reason not to do so and since she clearly knew what she was about, he hunkered down there and watched her set off towards the improbable structure below them.

It was the better part of an hour and a half before the girl returned, in the company of an older woman, also an Indian. This woman greeted Mellors in perfectly good English, saying, 'Thank you for what you have done. You are looking for one?'

Mellors got to his feet. It seemed slovenly and ungracious to sprawl on the ground while talking to a lady. He said, 'I'm looking for two men.'

'Tall Mexican? Half breed, with pocked face?'

'No,' said Mellors, his heart sinking, 'that ain't either of them.'

'Man with bright red hair like carrots? With one whose face is like a rat?'

This was such a succinct and accurate portrait of the two men whom he was hunting, that Chuck Mellors could not help but grin. He said, 'You surely got a way with words, ma'am. That's them for a bet. They over yonder?'

'Left this morning,' replied the woman.

'You know where they've gone?'

The woman paused for a few seconds, as she weighed up in her mind the possible losses and gains entailed in parting with this information. Jim Seward kept anything which came to his ears about the men frequenting his hotel to himself. He acted as though any snippets of gossip overheard were received

91

almost under the seal of the confessional. This reticence proceeded less from any powerful ethical code of which he might have been possessed and were more a matter of business sense. If once his clientele began to suspect that he was a man who couldn't keep his mouth shut, then at the very least, his business would drop off sharply. The case was quite different for the stable of girls he ran. They were sometimes able to profit from pillow talk: hearing of new opportunities, crimes that were planned, other cathouses in more pleasing locations and so on.

In the present case, the discussion between Red Halliday and Tom Jackson about their intended robbery of the Katy Flyer had been undertaken entirely, and unwittingly, in the presence of a woman who worked with a bounty hunter, selling him information which put him on the track of bandits and killers. The time and location of a train robbery was as marketable as gold dust to her. Notwithstanding, she felt that she owed the raggedy-looking stranger a debt for bringing her little friend safe through the territories and delivering her from an assailant, as she had been told. Not to mention where there was scarcely time for her to send word to anybody in time, before the robbery took place. Maybe she wasn't likely to make any profit on the information anyway. Finally, she said, 'You know what is the Katy Flyer?'

'Sure, it runs through this here district, 'tween Texas and Kansas.'

'The men you seek are going to rob it. Some way south of here is high ground. They call it Indian Hills. The train slows to climb. They mean to take it there, not tomorrow, but the next day. There, that's all.'

'I'm mightily obliged to you for your help, ma'am. I'm takin' it that you will look after this girl and that she's safe now?'

'That is so.'

'Tell me, does yon place sell food and drink? Maybe a bed for the night?'

'Yes. Don't follow us there. If we

93

meet there, don't know me. Wait here one hour after we go back.'

'Thank you. Thank you very much indeed.'

A curious circumstance was that Chuck Mellors never did learn what the young girl had been doing alone in the wilderness like that, nor the relation that she bore to the older woman. Although he stayed at the hotel for twenty-four hours, he never saw the girl again and had no idea at all whether she was on the premises or had moved on somewhere else. When he thought the matter over, his best guess was that the girl was either the baby sister of the woman who had given him such invaluable help and assistance or, and this was a less palatable notion, she was what one might term an apprentice whore. On balance, Mellors preferred to believe that she was some fallen woman's little sister whom he had brought to safety.

While Chuck Mellors was riding down towards Seward's Folly, the two men he was tracking down sat at their ease in a little lean-to which had been erected against a rocky cliff face. This structure had been used as a shelter for the men building the Missouri, Kansas and Texas Railroad, known to one and all as the KT or Katy. The Katy provided a vital link between Texas and the rest of the Union, carrying an enormous number of passengers and freight between Kansas and Texas. For this reason, it had, in the years following the end of the War Between the States, acted as something of a magnet for thieves, bandits and other low types. Some merely ran crooked poker games among respectable travellers, rooking them of their cash. Others committed robberies on board the trains and then leaped off at a convenient spot with the proceeds of their depredations. The most feared breed of men who preyed upon the Katy though were the train robbers; men who halted and robbed an entire train at gunpoint. A number of deaths had occurred as a consequence of this kind of crime.

So bad was crime getting on the Katy, that the directors were currently talking about employing armed guards, former soldiers and law officers, to ride shotgun on their trains. Some objected to the expense of such a proposal and in those July days, when Red Halliday, Jake Flint and Tom Jackson were about to hit the Katy Flyer, no agreement on the matter had yet been reached.

'You say we got to stay in this shithole for nigh on two days?' said Jake Flint, in a disgusted voice. 'What the hell was wrong with stoppin' on at Seward's place?'

'Because I want to make certain-sure that this goes according to plan,' replied Jackson. 'This way, we get to run through our parts and work out how it'll go. There's a train due in a couple o' hours and we can see how slow it goes up the slope here. We can figure out too, the most likely spot to jump it.'

Passenger train No. 2 had left Parsons promptly at ten that morning and was now thundering south towards the place where the three men were hiding out. Although to say that they were hiding out was stretching it a bit. Even when they were all huddled in the little shelter, anybody looking from the train window would have been able to see the three horses tethered outside the creosoted, wooden shack. It stood, after all, only a hundred yards from the track.

'I hope this don't turn out to be a snipe hunt, Tom,' remarked Halliday pleasantly enough. 'On account of me and my cousin here would be pretty ticked off about being confined here for two days and then not getting four thousand dollars each for our trouble.'

'You think I want to hole up here, either?' asked Jackson irritably. 'It's no picnic for me either, you know.'

'And you're sure you ain't talked to another living soul of this business?' said Halliday. 'Meaning that this fellow

97

as is moving his gold, won't have had the wind put up him or aught?'

'I picked up the tip from his sweetheart. I can't see where she'd go and tell him that she's a-cheatin' on him. And I ain't spoke of it to anybody else, neither.'

There was a silence for a minute or two, as each of the three men occupied themselves with their own, individual thoughts. The atmosphere was not what one might describe as cordial and Tom Jackson apprehended well enough that if his informant turned out to be mistaken, then at the very least he might expect to receive harsh words from Red Halliday and his cousin. For their parts, Halliday and Flint were beginning to ask themselves if they mightn't have taken a wrong turn by agreeing to trudge up here into the hills with a man neither of them cared for much. When all was said and done, they each had somewhere in the region of $1,500 coming to them when they cashed in those bearer bonds. Still, another $8,000 or so on top of that would come in very handy and so on balance, the game was probably worth the candle, providing always that Jackson's information was solid.

* * *

The man whom Halliday and Flint had embroiled, all unwitting, into being an accomplice to robbery and murder was having a somewhat more pleasant time of it than those stuck up by the railroad track at Indian Hills. Chuck Mellors was not in the habit of frequenting hotels and he found the experience of sitting in the lounge at Seward's Folly both novel and pleasing. Although he'd fought shy of breaking into the fifty dollars which he had been paid for his part in the killing of Richard Carstairs, regarding it as blood money, he justified the expenditure of some of that sum now on the grounds that the end justified the means. If he was to recover the $3,000 which was owed to the widow Carstairs and her child, then he would need to sustain himself in some way along the road to obtaining justice for the cruelly wronged family. So it was that Mellors felt to some extent that it was permissible to order a proper meal from Jim Seward and settle down at a table to enjoy it, even allowing himself the luxury of a bottle of porter set next to his plate.

★ ★ ★

While Mellors was relaxing and enjoying his meal, the Katy's passenger train No. 2 was puffing up the incline known as Indian Hills. From their vantage point by the cliff face, Halliday, Flint and Jackson watched closely as the locomotive struggled to draw its line of carriages up the slope to the plateau which then stretched pretty much all the way clear to Texas.

'It's slowed to a walking pace, that much I'll allow,' said Halliday. 'I can't see no reason why one of us shouldn't be able to haul his self up into the driver's cabin and get him to halt.' He turned to Jackson. 'What then? The other two make for the van?'

'That's the general idea,' replied Jackson. 'Get the guard to open the van and then take what we will.'

'How we goin' to know which of the boxes or bags in the van is the jewellery we's after?' enquired Jake Flint pertinently. 'You got any idea what this here gold will be wrapped like?'

'Not 'xactly,' said Jackson, 'but I reckon as those in the van'll know. We offer to kill one of 'em, I'll warrant that'll loosen they tongues.'

As they were talking, the men could see that the locomotive was making exceedingly heavy weather of the incline leading up to the plateau. For all the steam and noise it was generating, the train was, as Halliday had remarked, moving at barely more than walking pace. Another thought came to Halliday and he said to his companions, 'Say, that train's just 'bout able to haul up that slope with a good head of steam.

101

You know what I think? Once it comes to a stop, I shouldn't wonder if it wasn't to be stuck there. Starting on that steep slope looks to me a damned tricky undertaking.'

'So?' said his cousin. 'What's that to us?'

'Why, you fool, it means that after we finish a robbin' of it, then that train won't be in a fit state to go racing south to Denison to raise the alarm. Gives us more time to get clear, see?'

⋆ ⋆ ⋆

Living and working as he had in a wild part of the territories for three decades or so, Jim Seward reckoned that he had encountered most every type of strange individual and peculiar circumstance that the human race could produce. He was apt to say that nothing could surprise him any more. Despite this rash boast, Seward was forced to concede when telling the story later that in all his years running a hotel in such a barbarous and strange location, the first time that he had ever spied a man enter his establishment not only lacking pants, but drawers too, was that July afternoon that Chuck Mellors fetched up there.

The weary man had just finished his meal and had leaned back in the chair with a glass of ale about to be raised to his lips, when he heard Jim Seward, the man behind the bar, shout angrily, 'Hey, you can't come in here like that! What the hell's wrong with you?' Mellors turned to see the man whose possessions he had destroyed, standing at the entrance to the dining area, mother-naked from the waist down.

6

It was clear to anybody looking at the half-naked man standing there in the doorway, that he was very angry and that his anger was compounded with great embarrassment. His face was beet red, although whether from fury, shame or some combination of the two, it was impossible to say. One thing which Chuck Mellors noted with relief was that no gun-belt was in evidence. Since he'd wrecked the fellow's rifle, this gave him cause to hope that matters might pass off with no more than irate words being spoken. Even so, Mellors reached down unobtrusively and grasped the hilt of his pistol, easing back the hammer as he did so, until the weapon was cocked. Then he sat, half turned in his chair so that he could keep an eye upon the absurd figure upon whom everybody's attention was now focused.

Besides Mellors himself, there were five other people in the hotel lounge. Two were men, travellers like himself by the look of it, and sitting at the table with them were two women, one Indian and the other white. Then there was Jim Seward, standing behind the bar, trying to work out the best way of tackling this tricky situation.

'You hear what I tell you, fellow?' said Seward, loudly. 'You can't come in here like that. Where's your pants?'

'Some bastard burned them. Did the same for my saddle and other gear, too.'

'Well, I can't help that,' said Jim Seward, trying not to laugh. 'I'm sorry for your loss and all, but I still can't have somebody in your state of undress in here. Recollect, there are ladies present.'

If the amused looks on their faces were any indication, then the stranger had nothing on show that the 'ladies' hadn't seen before. The man glared venomously at the two women, who were now openly giggling at his

105

discomfiture and as he did so, his eye chanced to fall upon Mellors. His face turned from red to puce, before he exclaimed in a strangled voice, 'It's you, you son of a bitch! You're the one as done this to me.'

'Not but that you didn't right deserve it,' observed Mellors quietly. 'Tryin' to force yourself on an unwilling girl. Little more'n a child at that. Yeah, I burned your stuff and I'd do the same again.' He turned to the men sitting at the nearby table and said, 'This here's a rapist, or tried to be. I come across him out in the wilds, takin' advantage of a young girl. Ask him, don't take my word on it. He's damned lucky I spared his life.'

For a fraction of a second, the man was so taken aback at this, that he said nothing. The two men sitting near Mellors were staring at the half-naked man in disgust and he realized that he had lost any slight sympathy which his predicament might otherwise have earned him. Then he came charging across the room towards Mellors. Of course, the easiest way of dealing with the situation would have been to put a bullet through the fellow but Mellors didn't feel that this would be precisely fair. To have killed this rat when he'd been taken in the very act of trying to ravish a girl would have been one thing; to shoot him down now in cold blood, something else again.

In the usual way of things, Mellors was not at all averse to the odd rough-house and a little scrapping with his fists. The present situation, though, didn't really make anything of that sort a practical proposition. Suppose that he ended up being incapacitated by something as trifling as a sprained ankle, how then would he be able to bring those men to justice? All this had been going through Chuck Mellors's mind as soon as he saw who it was that had walked through the door. As the man hurtled towards him, he accordingly stood up and drew his pistol, intending to bluff the fellow into backing off. The sight of a drawn gun sometimes had the effect of cooling down a confrontation, especially when, as in the present case, one of the parties was seemingly unarmed.

Sadly, the man bearing down on Chuck Mellors was incandescent with rage and not accessible to either reason or the threat of imminent death. Ignoring the levelled pistol, he launched himself at Mellors, sending the two of them flying backwards. The stranger gripped Mellors in a fierce bear hug, presumably trying to prevent the gun from being brought up and used. As he did so, he began kicking at the other man's shins. Since he was wearing no shoes, this was a singularly ineffective fighting technique. Mellors was no weakling and managed to break the fellow's hold upon him. Still unwilling to kill him, he chose instead to slam the pistol against the side of his adversary's head, a tactic which in the past he had employed with a certain amount of success when wishing to subdue a determined opponent. In all the rush of action, he had, however, forgotten that his piece was cocked.

The result of pistol-whipping the man who was lying atop him caused great surprise to both Mellors and the fellow with whom he was wrestling. The piece went off at the first impact, the ball flying straight through the ceiling. For a moment, both of them were so taken aback by the sudden crash of gunfire that they paused in their struggle. It was the would-be rapist who recovered first from the shock, wresting the revolver from Mellors's grasp while he was still a little dazed by the unexpected sound of the shot. Having secured the pistol, the man leaped to his feet and, gripping the weapon with both hands, aimed it at Chuck Mellors's face. Lying there on his back, Mellors knew that he would be unable to rise before the man standing over him had got off at least one shot.

'Not looking so pleased with yourself now, are you, you bastard? You best get ready to die!' Having said which,

Mellors watched the fellow's forefinger whiten, as he tightened it around the trigger. Mellors closed his eyes and waited for the ball to take him between the eyes. When the roar of gunfire echoed through the room, he flinched, a little puzzled that he hadn't felt the half ounce of lead plough through his face and into his brains. He opened his eyes and the explanation dawned upon him.

The man without his pants lay dead on the floor. There was no sign of a wound, but Jim Seward was cradling a formidable squirrel gun, with which he had apparently killed the man who had been so intent on taking Chuck Mellors's life. Seward wasn't in the least degree averse to explaining how he had saved one man's life at the expense of another, saying, 'I never could stand those as takes advantage of helpless women. He didn't even trouble to deny it neither.' As Mellors got a little shakily to his feet, Seward continued, 'I keep this gun here expressly for when commotions like this break out. That cur didn't know as yours was a single action weapon. He just kept squeezing and squeezing the trigger, 'til he realized his error. Then, just as he'd figured out the case and was cocking the piece, I took him down with this.' He brandished the rifle and said, 'Straight through his ear at ten yards. That good shooting or what?'

Seward was clearly fishing for compliments and considering he had just saved his life, Mellors thought that the least he could do would be to flatter the hotel owner a little. He said, 'I never seen such sharp-shooting in the whole course o' my life. I'm eternally obliged to you, sir.'

'Well, that's fair enough. I guess I did pull your chestnuts out of the fire, or save your bacon, or put it how you will. Still, this ain't business. I can't have some dead rascal stretched out in my dining room. That won't answer. Tell me now, did this fellow come here on horseback?'

'I reckon as he must've. He wouldn't

have come here so fast, else.'

'Well then, that'll make life a mite easier. Lend a hand here and we'll heft him outside.' Seward called to the white girl sitting at the table with the two men and the Indian girl, saying, 'You there, Eulalie! Step lively and clear up any blood, there's a good girl.'

Grumbling a little, the woman stood up and went off, probably in search of a wash rag or mop. A circumstance that Mellors particularly noted was that not one of the four persons seated at the table had so much as batted an eyelid at the violent events which had taken place just a few feet from them. He guessed that this was one of those places where bloodshed and even sudden death was not an altogether remarkable happening.

Jim Seward took the arms and Mellors the ankles, and in that way, they carried the corpse out of the lounge and then through the lobby to the outside. There was to Mellors something peculiarly repugnant and distasteful about the whole enterprise. He found himself gazing at the private parts of the dead man and, despite the fact that he was plainly a villain, Mellors felt disturbed at the lack of dignity. Here had been a living, breathing being with thoughts, hopes and desires; now the two of them were bumping him about like he might have been a piece of meat.

Unceremoniously, Seward let drop his end of the burden and then said with satisfaction, 'Well, leastways he brought a mount with him. Happen he can depart in the same fashion.'

'I don't rightly understand you,' said Mellors.

'Wait here and you'll see. I'll be back directly.'

Mellors wondered briefly whether or not he should say a prayer or something, but then he thought that such an action would be a lot of foolishness. After all, he himself didn't even believe in the existence of the deity and the dead man surely hadn't comported himself like a Christian while he was alive.

Before he could follow this mental thread to its conclusion, Seward had returned with two lengths of rope.

'What's the game?' asked Mellors. 'You ain't a goin' to hang him?'

'Not a bit of it. Help me get him on his horse.'

'On his horse?'

'Yes, on his horse. Come on, you slow-poke. I want him out the way sooner rather than later. Wait up, though. Let's see if he's anything to pay for our trouble.'

'You mean to loot a dead body?' asked Mellors, a little taken aback. 'Why, I saw a fellow shot for robbin' a corpse during the war.'

'Well, this ain't the war, nor nothing like it,' said the eminently practical Seward. 'What d'you think we should do, advertise in the newspapers for his heirs and executors?' As he spoke, Seward's fingers were already diving into the dead man's shirt pocket and he gave a grunt of satisfaction. 'Well, just lookee here,' he said, waving something bright and shiny in his hand, 'four gold pieces. Ten dollar bits. Less'n you've any objections, we'll split 'em even, two each. That's fair, I suppose? Seeing as it was me as shot him.'

'I guess,' replied Mellors dubiously. 'It still don't somehow seem right.' Notwithstanding the pricking of his conscience, he took the proffered coins and slipped them into his own pocket.

It was a disagreeable and by no means inconsiderable job to hoist the corpse on to the palomino's back, and at one point Mellors recoiled in disgust when the dead man's genitals brushed against his hand. Seward said, 'You're a delicate one and no mistake. Stop acting like a girl and let's get this finished.' Once they had the man atop of his mount, the owner of the hotel lashed the dead man's wrists together and secured them to the bridle. Then he performed a similar office for the man's ankles, tying them together beneath the horse's belly.

Chuck Mellors watched all this curiously and then enquired, 'You fixin' just to send the horse on its way, bearing its late master?'

'That's about the strength of it. Why, you have any objections?'

Mellors shrugged his shoulders and said, 'I don't know. It seems a scurvy trick to play on the creature, leaving it burdened in that way with a corpse. It ain't done nothing to merit such treatment.'

The other man laughed and said, 'Oh, as to that, you needn't fret. Some Indian'll see this mount and be down on it in no time. After all, it's plain as a pikestaff that the rider's no longer in the land of the living. So long as our late friend's a good way from here by then, that's all that matters to me.'

Feeling reassured on this point and keen to try and forget his recent brush with death, Mellors suffered himself to be led back to the bar, Jim Seward having given it as his opinion that after all that, they could both do with a shot of strong liquor.

116

* ★ ★ ★

That night, the first that the three men planning to rob the Katy Flyer were to spend in the tumbledown shack next to the railroad line, was not an agreeable one for any of the parties concerned in the endeavour. Red Halliday and his cousin got on well enough in each other's company, but neither cared unduly for Tom Jackson. He, for his part, had only persuaded the other two men to join in the robbery because time was short and he didn't know where else to turn. These men would not have been his first choice for partners in such a business, not by a long chalk.

'What're you boys aimin' for to do with the cash we look to make from this?' asked Jackson, more to make conversation than because he really wanted to know.

'What's it to you?' replied Jake Flint. 'Nobody asked you 'bout your plans. It's enough that we'll do what's needful.'

117

'Hey, I didn't mean nothing,' said Jackson, 'just talking, you know?'

'Well then, don't,' said Halliday. 'To speak plain, we ain't precisely bosom friends and the only thing we got in common is wantin' four thousand dollars for a half hour's work.'

Tom Jackson was at first disposed to be affronted at being treated so disdainfully, but he soon recollected that he had given Halliday and that vicious cousin of his all the necessary information about the proposed robbery. He felt a creeping sensation of unease and a realization that those two men could just as well make an end to him and carry out the attack on the train by their own selves. It would not profit him a whit if he lost his life as a consequence of this scheme. So it was that he subsided and said nothing. An uneasy silence fell and all three men just lounged there smoking and staring out across the hills. Tom Jackson could not recall when last he had spent a more uncomfortable evening.

* ★ ★

For his part, Chuck Mellors was finding
the evening a very different kettle of
fish, and he was chatting in a friendly
fashion with the others who were staying at Seward's Folly. There were now
five men and four women in the dining
room besides Mellors and Seward, and
everybody was getting on famously. The
two men who had witnessed the killing
of the man with no pants, as they referred
to him, had been highly diverted by the
whole affair and after the corpse had
been disposed of, had invited Mellors to
come and sit at their table and tell the
full story. He did so, without mentioning the aftermath of the event; that is to
say, that the Indian girl he had rescued
had brought him to this very spot and
then more or less vanished.

For himself, Mellors had no desire to
enlarge upon what had brought him to
this out of the way spot. This reticence
was shared by the other men to whom
he talked; none of them said where they

had come from or where they might be headed. The most would be the odd remark such as, 'I was up Kansas way last fall' or 'Happen I'll head south in a bit'. He was no fool and Mellors sensed that these were men on the edge of the law. He was hardly in a position to cast the first stone though, seeing as he himself was technically on the run from a murder and he decided to give these fellows the benefit of the doubt and not enquire too deeply into what had led them here.

A man sitting opposite Mellors said, apropos of nothing in particular, 'I hear tell as the Katy's putting guards on their line soon.'

'The hell they are,' said another man. 'Where'd you hear that?'

'Ah you know,' replied the other vaguely, 'here and there. They say their directors are meeting about it this very week.'

'You're ahead of me with your information,' growled a third man. 'That'd queer a few pitches and no mistake!'

Mellors said nothing for a space, before asking casually, 'This ain't happening this very minute, is it? All this about guards on the railroad, I mean?'

This question provoked knowing looks and half smiles. The others at the table clearly had him marked down for a train robber. One said, 'Should be all right this week, fella, but were I you, I'd conduct any business you have with the Katy now, rather than later.'

The rest of the evening passed pleasantly enough, Mellors's casual enquiry about the presence of guards on the Katy's trains having been quite sufficient to reassure the others in the place that he was as crooked as they themselves.

That evening he spent in Seward's Folly was the only pleasant interlude for Chuck Mellors in his pursuit of the men who had caused him to become a fugitive. Aware though he was that the men sitting at the table drinking with him were thieves, rogues and most likely killers as well, he was able to relax, chat and take his ease. By the time he went to the bed he'd paid for, declining Seward's offer of a whore for the night, Mellors felt better about the world than he had done for some considerable while. He had twenty-five dollars in bills and change, along with the two ten dollar gold pieces. It was enough to tide him over for a month or more, even if he didn't find work in a hurry. There was tomorrow to get through, of course, but after that he could just get on his way and forget all about this bit of foolishness.

★   ★   ★

Tom Jackson was feeling far less contented and a great deal less optimistic about his future than Chuck Mellors. Truth to tell, he was fast becoming convinced that he'd taken a wrong turn in hitching up with Red Halliday and his cousin. Jackson had known well enough that they were a pair of mad bastards, he'd worked on a job with Halliday in the past, but there was something about the two of them on this expedition which was making Jackson profoundly uneasy. Still, he had been in a rush to rope in a couple of hands to assist him and they'd been the only men around. All the same, he took a long while to fall asleep that night, and when he did drift off into a slumber, his dreams were violent and confused.

7

The Katy Flyer was the pride of the Missouri, Kansas and Texas Railroad, the fastest and most luxurious train running through the territory of the Indian Nations which lay between Texas and Kansas. It was an express, which did not stop at all between Parsons in Kansas and Denison in Texas. It passed from one end of the territories to the other at top speed, halting for nothing. Most of the journey was across a vast, level plateau and the only place where the speed dropped to any noticeable degree was as the Katy Flyer climbed the slope leading south to the high plains which characterized that part of the country. It was at this spot, known locally as the Indian Hills, that Red Halliday and the others planned to ambush and rob the train.

In addition to providing a standard of

travel for passengers who would not be out of place in New York or Washington, the Katy Flyer also prided itself on its secure transit service — carrying packages and mail between Texas and Kansas. This was accomplished by means of a van at the back of the passenger coaches. It was a specially adapted and strengthened carriage, with a steel reinforced door and narrow slits to admit light, rather than proper windows. One clerk rode in the van, under strict instructions not to open the door for any reason until the proper destination was reached. During the journey, this clerk sorted the mail, thus ensuring swift onwards travel for the letters and parcels.

Most of the railroad trains running along the KT line stopped at various little way halts, which was generally where they were targeted by robbers. So fast was the Katy Flyer though, that nobody had yet attempted to rob her. Tom Jackson was not a deep thinker and it was only from hearing of the presence on board of that $12,000 worth of gold jewellery which had prompted him to launch this present enterprise.

★   ★   ★

The day dawned sunny and bright. As soon as Chuck Mellors opened his eyes, he had, against all reason, a good feeling about the day ahead. He felt powerfully that whatever else might befall him before dusk, he would not be breathing his last.

By stark contrast, Tom Jackson had precisely the opposite presentiment when he came to in that tumbledown shack leaning against the side of the cliff. For his part, a sense of dread enveloped him as soon as he became aware of his surroundings and remembered what he was planning to do that day. Red Halliday and his cousin Jake were fast asleep; their breathing regular, deep and even. Scripture tells us that 'morning brings counsel' and in this case, the advice that dawn seemed to have brought to Tom

Jackson was that there were worse things than losing out on a share of $12,000. What would it profit him to pocket $4,000 if he died a few hours later? It was when he put the thing into such terms that Jackson realized with a start that it was not the prospect of being killed in the course of the projected robbery which chilled his heart, but rather the fear of the two men he had roped in to help him.

Jackson got to his feet and moved stealthily towards the door of the hut. He was just lifting his hand to the latch when Jake Flint growled, 'Where you off to? Ain't a fixin' for to desert us, I'm hoping?'

Jackson's heart leaped into his mouth; he would have taken oath that both the other men were sound asleep. He said, 'Hell, I was only tryin' not to disturb the two of you. Just wanted to stretch my legs.'

Flint made no reply to this, which Tom Jackson took to mean that the other man had no objection to his leaving the place. Once outside, he filled his stubby clay pipe and lit it with a Lucifer, drawing the harsh smoke greedily into his lungs.

Jackson told himself that he had no especial reason to be nervous about the day's events. Lordy, he'd carried out enough robberies before! The more he thought matters over though, the more he realized that his fears centred less around the actual taking down of the Katy Flyer and had more to do with the two men he had engaged to assist him with the task. In short, he was less afraid of being shot by some passenger on the railroad train than he was of being harmed in some way by his partners.

His acquaintance with Red Halliday and Jake Flint was by no means an extensive one; he had once been part of a gang which included Halliday. They had only teamed up for a few days and Jackson had not had all that much to do with the man. Other than that, they came across each other from time to time in places such as Seward's Folly. Now that he was spending time alone with Halliday and his cousin, Tom Jackson could see what a pair of deadly rattlesnakes they were. He was more than half worried that they would carry out the ambush with him and then kill him afterwards, helping themselves to his share, as well as their own.

All of this was sobering and made him wonder if he shouldn't just give the whole business up as a bad job and simply dig up and get away from there. From behind him, he heard Red Halliday's voice, saying, 'You aimin' to brew up some coffee, man? I'm surely parched!' With both Red and Jake awake now, the moment had passed when he could have just slipped away. For good or ill, he was stuck with them for the rest of the day or at least until they'd robbed that blamed train. He'd just have to watch his back was all.

★　★　★

129

Chuck Mellors was having an altogether more agreeable time that morning. Jim Seward was up early and, seeing as all his guests were leaving that day, had deigned to fry up a load of eggs and brew a gallon of black coffee so strong you could float a spoon on it. Seward had taken a liking to young Mellors and was disposed to be chatty with him. When the other men were out of earshot, Seward said, 'Mind if I ask where you're heading?' This was not the sort of question that he would, in the usual way of things, have dreamed of asking anybody availing themselves of his facilities, but something told him that Chuck Mellors was not a run-of-the-mill villain or shady character of the kind who generally fetched up there.

'I've a little business to attend to, not far from here,' said Mellors guardedly, 'but there's no mad hurry.'

'Listen,' said Seward, leaning forward a little and lowering his voice so that those at the table across the bar room would not be able to hear him, 'if you're fixin' to interfere with the Katy Flyer, then don't be doing of it. They haven't yet got guards on it, but I heard where there's a sharpshooter been engaged, with instructions to take out anybody who tries any funny business. You hear what I'm tellin' you?'

'Lord,' replied Mellors, astounded that anybody might see him in the character of a train robber, 'I've no designs upon holding anybody up! I don't come over like that, surely?'

'I'm just letting you know what's what, that's all,' said Jim Seward. 'No offence meant, I'm sure.'

'None taken, sir. Now I been read as a bounty killer and a train robber! Whatever will people mistake me for next?'

★ ★ ★

Tom Jackson faced the unappealing prospect of making small talk with a couple of men he fancied might be planning to murder him and this had the effect of making his conversation that morning stilted and jerky. Red noticed this and said at one point, 'You's jumpier than a cat this day, Jackson. What ails you, man?'

'Nothing, just thinking about tonight's job is all.'

Jake Flint chipped in at this point, remarking, 'You need to relax more, you know? I'm getting nervy just watching you. You sure you ain't scared of aught?'

'No, man. Not a damned thing.'

'Well then,' said Red Halliday, who had moved around behind Jackson while he was talking to Flint, 'you ought to be.' Having delivered himself of this opinion, Halliday looped a noose of rope over Tom Jackson's head from behind and then proceeded to strangle him.

Jackson's first impulse was to reach up and try to relieve the pressure on his throat by tugging at the rope, but this didn't answer. Then he reached for his pistol, but Jake Flint was too quick for him, diving in and snatching the gun from the holster and tossing it clear.

By this time, Jackson's face was purple and he was kicking his legs wildly, trying

132

to get some purchase, so that he could lever himself free of Red Halliday's noose. However, his strength was waning and after another few seconds, the vigorous kicking subsided and became little more than aimless and convulsive twitching. In his final extremity, the dying man fouled himself, which caused Halliday to thrust the corpse from him in disgust.

'I thought the bastard would never die,' said Halliday, a little breathless from his exertions. 'Lend me a hand here to shift him well out the way. I don't want him lying here, stinkin' the place out like that.' Those few brusque and uncaring words were all the eulogy and epitaph which Tom Jackson was destined to receive. Few noticed his absence in the coming months and within a year, he might never have lived, for all the thought that was given to him.

It had indeed been Red Halliday and Jake Flint's intention all along to murder the man who had put them on to this present job. Four thousand dollars is

$4,000 and both of them thought that Jackson's share of the proceeds was better in their pockets than in his. They were also confident that what three determined men might accomplish in the robbery line, so might two. Once the calculation had been undertaken in this way, Tom Jackson's life was as good as over already, of which fact he had perhaps somehow felt a premonition.

After the body of the late Tom Jackson had been hidden behind a pile of rocks, some distance from the lean-to, the cousins fell to discussing how they would undertake the theft of the jewellery from the Katy Flyer.

'Seems to me,' said Halliday, 'we'll both be needed when we visit that van and try to get them to open up. Can't have one of us wasting time with the driver up in the locomotive.'

'You think we should kill the driver? What about the fireman or stoker or whatever you call him?' asked Jake Flint. ' 'Sides which, if we can get by without killing, I'd sooner.'

'You going soft?'

If any other person on the face of the earth, excepting his cousin, had made such a suggestion, he would swiftly have been disabused of such a fanciful notion. As it was, Flint gave his cousin a cold look and said, 'I'll kill any man, woman or child that takes breath, if it'll profit me. As you know. But in this case, the killing of someone employed by the Katy is going to bring us more trouble than we need. There'd be big rewards, posses, bounty hunters and I don't know what all else to contend with. Don't let me hear talk about anybody going soft again.'

Close as the two men were, Red Halliday sensed that he might perhaps have stepped too close to the edge and said hastily, 'You know I meant nothin' by it. Happen you're right anyway. If we just steal some gold, that's one thing. Murder's another.' As it chanced the two men were, despite their agreement, fated to commit murder within twelve hours. It was not to be the driver of the

135

locomotive who fell victim to them though and the killing was quite unplanned.

* * *

Chuck Mellors parted on good terms with the owner of the cathouse and never saw him again. Jim Seward, still not able to make out what the young man was about, gave him directions to the Indian Hills, never asking what his purpose was in heading that way. Seward knew full well that the Katy ran along that way, but that was no affair of his.

From all that he was able to collect, Chuck Mellors figured that he would get to the Indian Hills in four hours or so. From what the Indian woman had told him, the two men he was after and their companion were expecting a railroad train to pass through there at about four that afternoon, which meant that he had a couple of hours in hand to see what was what. The truth of the matter was that Mellors had not yet decided what he would do when he caught up with the men who had caused him to be a party to robbery and murder. Sometimes he thought that he would shoot the pair of them and then take those bonds back to Perseverance and see if he could get them to Richard Carstairs's widow. Then again, he might end up being hanged if he did that. Other times, he had it in mind to confront the two of them and ask, man to man, why they had behaved as they did. Mellors was, however, not so sanguine as to expect that they would respond to such an appeal. Every scheme he turned over in his mind seemed to have an awful lot of drawbacks and yet here he was now, likely to catch up with the men before nightfall.

By noon, Chuck Mellors had come up with a tentative plan for handling matters if and when he caught up with the men who had caused him to be in this unenviable position of being on the run for a murder of which he was quite guiltless. He would draw nigh to them, with his pistol out and ready for action and then invite them to throw down the bonds which they had stolen, so that Mellors could return them to the woman who was now penniless. That was his chief aim now — to alleviate the suffering of the widow and her child. He'd find a way to send the money to Mrs Carstairs and then later on perhaps provide information against the men who had carried out the crime. If they simply surrendered those documents, well then, he'd let them go on their way; aye, least for now. The main thing was to get justice for that poor widow.

Even as he was reasoning the matter out in his mind, Mellors knew deep within that this was not likely to be how the business resolved itself and that the chances of those two scoundrels just rolling over and doing as he bid them were negligible. There would be blood shed before this little episode spun itself out to the end.

* ★ * ★ * ★

Hector Grant's father had been a classical scholar who had named his son after the Trojan prince in Homer's Iliad. He little could have suspected when arranging for his son to be christened, twenty-nine years earlier, that his first-born boy would turn out to be not a college lecturer or something of that sort, but a bounty killer. When the great War Between the States broke out in 1861, Hector Grant had answered Mr Lincoln's call for volunteers and went off to join the Union Army. This decision was actuated less by any detestation of slavery as an institution, still less because he was anxious to give his life to preserve the Union. It was more the case that he had, despite his cultured upbringing, never been a bookish type; he far preferring hunting, fighting and shooting. When the war came to an end, Grant was twenty-three years of age and quite unable to settle down to a normal, peaceful life.

There were a number of young men like Hector Grant in the years following the signing of the instrument of surrender at Appomattox in the spring of 1865. Men who were restless and couldn't seem to settle to any occupation that did not involve guns. Some fought in the Indian Wars, others became lawmen or took up as outlaws. A few, like Grant, drifted into working as bounty hunters. These were men who tracked down fugitives and wanted men, and then handed them over to the law for the reward money. Transporting a vicious criminal for miles across rough and largely lawless territory was a mortal hazard, which was why a few such men (Hector Grant was one) preferred to kill their quarry and then collect on the corpses. It was less risky that way.

The owners of the Missouri, Kansas and Texas Railroad Company, known to one and all as the Katy, were anxious both to discourage attacks on their trains and to save their shareholders' money. Before going to all the expense of paying regular salaries for armed guards to ride shotgun on their services, somebody had come up with the luminous idea of offering free travel and a small honorarium to a half dozen or so men who might see this as a business opportunity. The plan being that if each of their trains had a bounty hunter on board and it was made clear to these men that if they killed any bandits who were menacing the Katy's services, then the railroad would happily transport the bodies of their victims to the next town where they could pick up any rewards on offer, and that might act as more of a discouragement to potential robbers than any number of retired police officers wishing to supplement their pensions by acting as guards.

Jim Seward had caught wind of this enterprise, due to a remote cousin of his being in the bounty hunting line of work and having been offered the chance to come through the territories in this way. It was this which led him to tip the wink to Chuck Mellors earlier that day.

Everybody's plans and stratagems were thrown into disarray by the discovery, just before the Katy Flyer left Parsons that day, of a cracked pipe in the locomotive's boiler. It would have been madness to risk a non-stop run through the Indian Territories with such a defect and so for two hours, the passengers cooled their heels at the depot while a team of engineers worked frantically to fix the defect. Hector Grant, who had a marked weakness for strong liquor, spent those two hours in the bar attached to the railroad depot; first supping porter and then rye whiskey. He had already had a few drinks that morning so by the time everything was ready and he stumbled aboard the train, he was as drunk as a fiddler's bitch and promptly fell asleep, before the Katy Flyer had even pulled out of Parsons. As a consequence of this, Grant slumbered like a baby through some of the crucial events which took place a few hours later.

Red Halliday and Jake Flint began, as the afternoon wore on, to despair of the

$12,000 which they now believed to be their due. It was looking as though they had committed murder for nothing. Just as they were preparing to pull out and ride south, Halliday happened to glance across the plain below and saw in the distance the plume of white steam which signalled the presence of a locomotive. He hollered in jubilation and shouted to his cousin, 'Jake, I reckon as we're in business after all!'

'Thank Christ for that,' growled Flint profanely, 'I'd've have hated to think we spent all this time out here for naught. We best mount up.'

The two men had agreed that the best scheme would be for them to threaten to kill the driver unless he brought the train to a halt, and then to march him and the fireman back to the guarded van at the rear of the train, to prevent either of them from trying to start the locomotive moving again until they had completed their depredations. Although neither of them said so out loud, it had struck both Halliday and

Flint that an extra pair of hands wouldn't have come amiss on this expedition and they were wondering if they might not have done better to let Jackson stay alive and help with the robbery before killing him. Still, there was nothing to be done about it now so they would just have to make the best of matters and manage the job without him.

* * *

On a rocky crag above the men who were intending to take down the Katy Flyer, Chuck Mellors had what might not inaptly be termed a 'bird's eye view' of the whole scene. Right below him, he could see those who had wronged him, seated on their horses. Away in the distance, he could make out the railroad train, chugging away towards them, fast approaching the incline which led up to the high plateau which stretched all the way from here to Texas.

As soon as he had arrived in the vicinity, Mellors had at once seen that his idea of approaching those killers and holding any kind of discussion with them would have been a non-starter; they'd have shot him down before he even got close enough to open his mouth. Once he was close enough to the Indian Hills to see the railroad line gleaming in the sun, Mellors had dismounted and led the mare slowly up to his present vantage point to spy out the lie of the land. He saw at once that his quarry were as edgy as could be and that it would have been madness to ride straight at them, however pacific his intentions. So he waited and formulated a new plan. He would wait until they were otherwise occupied and then he might be able to get close enough to challenge them and ask for the bonds which they had stolen.

Of course, if Chuck Mellors had been a little more worldly and experienced in the ways of bad men, he would have known that bracing a dangerous criminal while he was in the course of committing a capital crime would not be a whit less hazardous than riding up to the same man while he was idling and smoking. In fact, it would be a good deal worse, because during the actual commission of crimes, the nerves of such men tended to be screwed up to such an exquisite pitch, that they would fire at the least unwelcome or even unexpected circumstance. But there it was, Mellors had had few previous dealings with such men and could judge them only by his own standards of behaviour.

8

At first, everything went just swimmingly for the men robbing the Katy Flyer. The driver was only too ready to apply the brakes and bring the train to a juddering halt on the steep slope leading up to the plateau, notwithstanding the fact that he was wondering how the deuce he would be able to get it moving again up the incline without any of the momentum previously gained through thundering across the level ground below. Howsoever, his only present interest was in the preservation of his life, and when ordered at the point of Red Halliday's gun to bring the mighty machine to a stop, he did so without demur. The fireman similarly evinced no wish to die in defending the interests of the Kansas, Missouri and Texas Railroad Company and followed the driver's lead in doing as he was bid.

While Halliday was leading the two men from the locomotive's cabin towards the rear of the train, where they would not be able to get up to any mischief, like getting the train moving again, Jake Flint had hoisted himself up onto the coupling which linked the secure van to the next carriage and began hammering on the door to gain admission. It was immediately clear to him that under no circumstances at all would the clerk inside the van accede to his demands to open the door.

'You can holler all you like out there,' said the clerk stoutly, 'but I ain't opening this door and that's a fact. You might as well leave now.'

Although neither Flint nor Halliday knew it, the van was lined on the inside with steel plates which rendered it well proofed against any firearm. It would take a keg of fine-grained powder to open that little truck unless it were to be unlocked from within.

While increasingly heated shouted exchanges were taking place between Jake

Flint and the fellow in the armoured van, Hector Grant continued to snore gently. If he had been a uniformed and armed employee of the railroad company, of course, some passenger might have woken him up and alerted him to the fact that a robbery was probably in progress. In fact, though, Grant looked just like any other traveller and there was nothing to indicate that he was really a famed bounty hunter.

On the rock overlooking the unfolding drama, Chuck Mellors was getting to his feet and walking back down the slope to his horse. He figured that now was the right time to have a word with those two villains so he mounted up and began trotting down towards the train.

When Red Halliday turned up at the secure van with his two captives, he was slightly appalled to find that Flint had not yet gained access to the valuables. He said, 'What are you thinkin' of, man? I'd have expected you to be in by now.'

'The bastard won't open the door,' shouted Jake Flint furiously, 'you try your luck!'

The driver, an old man of sixty or more, smiled at this and observed with some satisfaction, 'Don't look to me like your luck's in today, boys. You're like to leave empty-handed.'

'Shut up, you stupid old fool,' said Flint, 'or I'm apt to put a ball through your head.'

The driver, who was a tough old veteran of two wars, replied, 'That won't get you in the van.'

The driver's remark gave Halliday an idea and he said, 'Get up there, old timer, up by my partner there, nigh to the door of that damned van.'

The driver climbed carefully up, until he stood next to Flint. Red Halliday then shouted to the clerk inside the van, 'You don't open that door, we're goin' to kill your driver stone dead, you hear what I say?'

There was a long pause, before the clerk said, 'Sorry, Mr Brodie, but the regulations say I'm still not to unlock this door.'

'That's fine, son,' the driver assured him loudly, 'you do as you've been told.'

This exchange between the clerk in the van and the locomotive driver angered Jake Flint a great deal, for it showed that firstly, killing the old man would be pointless, because it wouldn't help open up the van and secondly, that the driver was an awkward bastard who was determined to frustrate their plans if he was able. Flint accordingly gave the man an almighty shove, which sent him flying down to the ground, breaking his arm as he fell.

Halliday said, 'Keep watch on this one,' pushing forward the fireman, 'and wait here.' He sprinted off down the train and returned less than two minutes later with a young and scared woman.

Cocking his pistol, Red Halliday pointed it straight at the woman's face and said, 'Now beg for your life. Nice and loud, so that fellow in the van can hear you.' Whereupon the woman did better than that; she began screaming hysterically for help.

Flint shouted to the clerk, 'You hear that? We goin' to kill that lady in ten seconds, you don't open up this door.'

This time, there was no defiant reply from the van and this gave Halliday and Flint cause to suppose that their latest gambit might be about to succeed. Then two things happened more or less simultaneously. Halliday saw a rider coming down towards the train and no sooner had he noticed this, than a shot rang out. Somebody further up the train had opened fire on him. Then the woman he was holding struggled round and bit his hand. He whipped his pistol across her face and, as she fell to the ground, Halliday lashed out with his boot, catching the woman in the throat.

There was another shot from up towards the engine and Jake Flint leaned round the corner of the carriage and fired back in that general direction. The fireman, seeing how the woman passenger had been treated and feeling revulsion, mingled with unreasoning anger, jumped at Red Halliday and attempted to wrestle him to the ground, whereupon Halliday shot him twice. There came another shot, this time from the man on horseback and, realizing that they were fated not to get into the van, both Halliday and Flint ran to their horses, firing back at both the rider and the carriage from which the other shots appeared to have come.

If Hector Grant had been either sober or not just have been awoken from his slumbers, the whole business would have been resolved forever, then and there. He was a deadly shot and firing from cover like this at fleeing targets was the game he liked best. But there it was, he had been drunk when he dozed off and there was more than enough liquor circulating through his veins to spoil his aim and he was still a little groggy from being woken up before he'd had a chance to sleep off his over-indulgence at the Parsons depot. None of his shots came within six feet of either of the bandits. As for Chuck Mellors, he hadn't been aiming at the men when he fired. He had seen the woman being hit and fired over the heads of the group. With everybody bunched up so close together, it would have been madness to hope that he would be able to hit one of those people, rather than another, at a distance of fifty feet or so.

It was at times like these that Chuck Mellors's gentlemanly instincts sometimes led him to make the wrong decision when it mattered greatly. Seeing those scamps ride off, his first impulse was to race after them and deal with them promptly and sharply. Set against this was the fact that he had seen a woman struck down and nobody seemed to be tending to her or even seeing how badly she might be hurt. So instead of pursuing the fugitives, Mellors urged on his horse to the rear of the railroad train to see what assistance he might be able to render to the lady he had just seen handled so roughly.

He could see, even before he got down from his horse, that there was nothing to be done for the man who had been shot. He lay there in that peculiarly ungainly and awkward pose which only corpses seem able to adopt. The woman wasn't moving either, but Mellors had hopes that in her case it might be merely a faint. He walked towards her and then stopped dead in his tracks as a voice behind him said, 'Take another step, you son of a bitch, and you're a dead man!'

When he realized that at least two of the men who had apparently held up the Katy Flyer were escaping, Hector Grant was overwhelmed with fury at his stupidity. He knew that this trip had been an opportunity to get his feet under the table at the railroad company and who knew where it might lead? A permanent post, protecting the trains travelling through the territories? Setting up in an outfit like Pinkerton's? And now, because of his own foolish weakness, he had thrown those chances in the gutter. Wondering if there was anything to be retrieved from the mess, Grant stood up and made his way down the carriage. When he got to the end, he opened the door and hopped down. At once, he saw that one of the robbers was still on the scene. For some reason, he hadn't fled with his accomplices. Well, one man captured was better than nothing. Hector Grant raised his pistol and shouted a challenge.

How a shooting match didn't develop at that point is something of a mystery, because two men faced each other with guns in their hands, each convinced that the man in front of him was a ruthless bandit. Had it not been for the frantic shouting of passengers leaning out of windows, then at least one and possibly both men would have died that afternoon. People yelled at Hector Grant things such as, 'He weren't one of 'em. He was shooting at 'em', and 'Not him, you fool, he ain't a robber!' From which Mellors apprehended that the man in front of him was some kind of lawman. For his part, Grant understood that the other man had not taken part in this damned robbery which he had been unable to prevent.

It was Chuck Mellors who ended the confrontation by saying, 'You goin' to use that pistol or are you posing to have your picture painted or something?'

For a moment, things might have gone either way, but then Grant laughed shortly and said, 'Happen we're at cross purposes. I thought you was one of them as just attacked us.' He replaced his pistol in the holster, whereupon Chuck Mellors did the same thing and everybody watching began to breathe a little easier.

The two men went over to see what aid they might be able to offer to the lady who was lying by the side of the track. Grant went up and touched her throat lightly, feeling for a pulse. He turned to Chuck Mellors and said, 'She's gone.'

At first, Mellors didn't rightly understand the other and asked stupidly, 'What d'you mean, she's gone?'

'She's dead,' said Grant impatiently,

'she must have got an unlucky blow to her neck, broke it. Look!' He waggled the dead woman's head from side to side, demonstrating how it moved more like part of a marionette with the strings cut than any human body you ever saw.

'That's about enough of that,' said Mellors, horrified. 'You mean those brutes killed a defenceless woman?'

'That's about the strength of it, yeah.'

By this time, other passengers had got down from the train and were coming to stare at the two dead bodies. The driver said, 'I think my arm's bust, but if we can get a sling, I might be able to manage something in the driving line. If the fire hasn't died down yet, which ain't likely. They do for Pete?'

'Pete's the fireman, yeah?' asked Hector Grant.

'Yeah.'

'Well, they done for him, same as the woman.'

'Lord a mercy,' said the driver, 'but they were a rare pair of villains.'

'You got that right,' said Mellors

slowly, 'I reckon I'm goin' for to ride after them now. I hope you folk manage all right.'

This proposal was very far from being all right with one of those present, namely, Hector Grant. In the first place, he was desperately anxious to redeem himself in the eyes of the Kansas, Missouri and Texas Railroad Company, and the best way that he could see of achieving that end was to track down and bring back, dead or alive, the men who had attacked the train. Surely the bosses of the railroad line would not be unmindful of the man who took such an action? Secondly, he wondered if those two men were wanted elsewhere. There might be a double reward in the case, if so.

So it was that when Chuck Mellors announced his intention of riding after the men who had tried to rob the train, Grant looked at him suspiciously and said, 'You a bounty man too?'

'Nothing of the kind,' said Mellors, 'I got business with those as done this.'

'What business?'

'I reckon that's my affair. It don't concern you nor anybody else.'

Grant recognized a steely determination in this man and knew that there was no purpose in trying to talk him out of his plan. Instead, he said, 'Wait 'til I open up the horse box and we'll go together. Two'd have a better chance than one.'

Mellors looked at the bounty hunter and said, 'You ain't the law, are you?'

'No, but I have an interest in those two, same as you.'

They stared at each other for a space, weighing up the situation. It was fairly plain that neither of them were going to back down and at last Chuck Mellors said, 'Well, get your horse then. But make haste or we'll lose 'em.'

'They'd have to fly to avoid me tracking them down,' said Grant and he managed to make this sound not like some extravagant boast, but more in the nature of a sober statement of unvarnished fact.

The dead man and woman were loaded reverently onto the train and the old driver, his smashed wrist supported in a makeshift sling, was helped back into the cab. One of the conductors was persuaded to strip to his shirtsleeves and play the part of stoker until they reached Denison. Seeing that things were arranged, after a fashion, Hector Grant set off with Chuck Mellors to track down the men who had committed two such senseless murders.

As they rode south, Grant said, 'I don't mind that you haven't told me yet what your interest is in those fellows.'

'I don't recall your telling me why you want to catch them neither, if it comes to that.'

Grant chuckled and said, 'Well, that's fair enough. I'm hoping for a job with the Katy, the railroad company, you know. Your turn to lay down, now.'

Chuck Mellors thought for a while and then, when it was starting to look as though he was not going to answer, he said, 'Those men have something which belongs to a widow and her children. I aim to take it from them and restore it to the rightful owner.'

'You kin to the wronged party or something?'

'No.'

And that was all that Mellors could, either then or later, be induced to say on the subject. Grant thought to himself after hearing this that there was something that his companion was excessively anxious should not come out and determined that before this game had run its course, he would find out what that was.

He was no tracker himself, but even Mellors was able to see the hoof prints of the riders they were following. Not many people came down this way, other than on the railroad, and the tracks were clear and sharp. For a while, the trail ran alongside the line to Denison, but then veered off to the left, leading, from all that he could make out, up into a range of hills.

'This the way?' Mellors asked,

indicating the way up the slope.

'Yes, but we'll need to be a little cautious. Those boys have slowed down now and might even be waiting for us, up yonder.'

'You can tell that from those prints?' asked Mellors in surprise.

'No, you damned fool. They went galloping off from that train an hour and a half since. They couldn't keep up that pace for long. They're like us now, just trotting. Tracks don't tell you everything, you got to use your brain, too.'

By the time Mellors and Grant reached the crest of the hills which overlooked the plateau, their horses were just about ready to rest for a space. The two men dismounted and stretched their legs. It is often the case when making your way up mountains or hills, that every time you think that you've got to the top, there is another and higher point just ahead. So it was now, with the flat ground that they were currently on leading away into the distance to another and higher range of craggy little peaks. There were still a few hours of daylight left, but it seemed to Chuck Mellors that they would be needing to make some plans if they hadn't caught up with those men by nightfall. He expressed this idea tentatively to Grant, who responded by saying, 'Well, if it accords with your own wishes, I reckon we ought to carry on 'til the moon rises and then snatch some sleep. If there's going to be gunplay and hard riding, I'd as soon it took place in broad daylight, you hear what I'm saying?'

'You don't want to try and creep up and ambush them while they're sleeping?'

'I do not. All that business when you tiptoe up to some outlaw in the dead of night and then catch him unawares is a lot of foolishness. Those boys sleep with one eye open and the only thing we're like to get from it is a ball through our bellies before we get within twenty feet of them. No, I'd sooner take them in a fight. It's less trouble in the long run, trust me.'

While he was making this speech,

Hector Grant could see that the other man was eyeing him curiously. He said, 'What's wrong, I got a smut on my nose or something?'

'No,' replied Mellors, 'I was just wondering what this job is that you was hoping to get with the Katy. Way you talk, you sound like a bounty killer.'

'What's it to you? We both want to catch those two men, what do you care who I am or why I want 'em?'

'It's nothing to me. Just recollect though that when we catch up with them, I want the bearer-bonds that they're carrying. What you do with them boys after that is your affair.'

At the words 'bearer-bonds', Hector Grant's ears pricked up and he suddenly realized that he knew what was going on here, or at least part of it. It came to him that there would be a double reward for those men once he had caught them, and it also crossed his mind that there might be another one for the pot, so to speak, in the man he had picked up with that afternoon. It was part of Grant's stock-in-trade to know who was wanted and what they were wanted for in the districts which he frequented.

In his saddle bag, Grant had a collection of newspaper cuttings and Wanted bills. Somewhere among them, and it was, he was convinced, a recent item, something referring to a man with flaming red hair and mentioning bearer-bonds. As he mulled this over, Hector Grant recollected something else. Was there not something said in the same news item about two accomplices in that case, one of whom was described as 'a mountain of a man'? He sneaked a quick look at the man riding beside him and concluded that this fellow might very easily have been the one seen with the red-headed man and another. The description of 'a mountain of a man' definitely fitted his travelling companion. Had he fallen out with his friends and been cheated of the spoils? The more he considered the matter, the more it looked to Grant as though he might well end up with three suspects to collect on. He tried to remember what had been offered for those mixed up in the theft of the bearer-bonds, but found he couldn't recollect the amount off hand. He'd have to look in his bag and refresh his memory when he was not being watched.

9

There were sound practical reasons for halting their pursuit for the night, quite apart from Hector Grant's dislike of trying to surprise an enemy in the dark. The hills through which they were passing were a regular warren of little chasms and tiny, rocky defiles. The place was a maze and tracking the men who they were seeking would have been all but impossible once the sun had set. There was a new moon that night, with scarcely enough light to recognize a man's face, even if he was sitting opposite you. Distinguishing the spoor of one horse or another would be out of the question. Then again, it would hardly have helped their quest if one of their horses lamed itself in the dark.

It would have been madness to advertise their presence by lighting a fire so, after untacking the horses, Mellors and

Grant simply rested themselves by leaning against boulders and reflecting on how hungry they were. There was little to be done about it and after agreeing that they could both surely do with a steak or something, they changed the topic of conversation, which then stumbled rapidly to a halt. Neither man felt inclined to explain why he was really hunting down the men who had tried to rob the train and neither was at all bothered about showing his distrust of the other. By common consent therefore, they agreed to turn in and be up early to see if they couldn't run their quarry to earth.

* * *

Red Halliday and Jake Flint were pretty ticked off after their bungled attempt to knock over the Katy Flyer. They tended to blame the man they had murdered for the debacle. As Flint said, 'If that fool Jackson hadn't've got us mixed up in this, we'd be in Texas by now.'

'Ain't that the truth?' replied his

cousin bitterly. 'I wish we'd not listened to that jackass. You think anybody'll be on our tail for it?'

Halliday thought this over and then said, 'Him that turned up and started shooting. I mind I seen him before somewhere. Damned if I know where, though.'

'You think he's the law?'

'Didn't have that feel about him. Wish I could remember where I seen him, though.'

It was fairly typical of the two cousins that although they had only a few days ago embroiled an innocent man in a murder and robbery, they cared so little for those they used that already this latest victim of their predatory lifestyle evoked no recollection in either of them. Perhaps it was because it is hard to judge a man's height so easily when he is mounted. Had they seen Chuck Mellors close up and on foot, his very size might have served to jog their memories.

Like the men who were in pursuit of them, Halliday and Flint decided to sleep almost as soon as darkness fell and then make an early start at dawn. Even if they were not presently being hunted, it was a matter of common sense that the wider the distance you put between yourself and a robbery or murder, the better it was likely to be for you.

*   *   *

The first person to awake the following morning was Hector Grant and after ascertaining that his new partner was still sound asleep, Grant rummaged around until he found the sheaf of news cuttings and bills upon which so much of his work was based. There were two items relevant to this present case. One was a piece from *The South Kansas Plain Dealer*, which told the story of a robbery and brutal murder. This had alerted Grant and caused him to contact the sheriff's office in Topeka. The reward now stood at $200 a head for the three men. He looked with new interest at the fellow with whom he had picked up yesterday, seeing him now as being worth cash money at some point, assuming of course that Grant's suspicions were well-founded.

It was while he was being scrutinized in this way that Mellors opened his eyes and growled, 'What for are you staring at me in that way?'

'No reason at all,' said Hector Grant hastily, 'I was just thinking that the sooner we are on our way, the better.'

'That's what you're thinking,' said Mellors, sitting up and reaching for his boots, 'I wonder you didn't shake me or something, 'stead o' just looking at me like that.'

'Well, you're awake now. Let's be moving.'

Chuck Mellors looked at the other man and for a moment, it looked as though he were on the verge of speaking. Then he gave an almost imperceptible shrug and pulled on his boots. The atmosphere between the two of them could not have been described as cordial and indeed, it was increasingly plain that neither of them trusted the other. It made sense for them to stay together until they had taken down the men who tried to rob the Katy Flyer, but what would happen after that was anybody's guess.

*   *   *

Red Halliday was disturbed from his slumbers by the sound of speaking. Living as he did, on the edge of the law, Halliday was accustomed to coming to and being ready for action at a second's notice. He sat up at once on waking and listened to the brief exchange which followed. When first he awoke, he had half wondered whether or not it was voices from a dream which had caused him to wake up, but as he sat there, the true explanation dawned on him. He and his cousin Jake were in a little, blind gully surrounded on three sides by sheer rock walls about eight or ten feet high. The mountains through which they had been making their way when night over-took them were hatched and cross-cut with tiny canyons and gullies, like that in which they were presently sheltered. It sounded as though at least two men were situated just a matter of a few yards away, most probably in a similarly sheltered spot.

Being careful not to make any noise at all, Halliday crept over to where Flint was snoring and shook his shoulder, keeping a hand poised over his cousin's mouth to clamp over it and stifle any sound, if need be. When Jake Flint opened his eyes, Halliday put his finger to his lips to indicate silence and then leaned forward, whispering, 'Keep perfectly still. There's someone near at hand.'

Flint nodded slightly, to show that he understood. Halliday crawled over to where their guns were lying and picked up both pistols. Then he carried them over to Flint and handed him his own weapon. Carefully and slowly, so that there should be no sharp and distinctive sounds which might echo from the rock faces, both Halliday and his cousin cocked their pieces and then turned to face the opening which led to the place where they had been sleeping. Both men hoped devoutly that their horses would remain quiet for the next few minutes. In complete silence, Red Halliday and Jake Flint both sat there, their pistols cocked, watching to see if anybody were about to approach them. After five minutes or so, they heard the jingling of bridles and clip-clopping of hoofs on bare rock; sounds which slowly receded into the distance. They began to breathe easy again.

'You think they was looking for us up here?' asked Flint.

'Maybe. Let me scoot up yonder and see if I can see anything. If there's a posse been raised, we need to know what's what.'

'A posse? There's been no time for such a thing.'

'No, that's what I woulda thought, too.'

Halliday left the gully and clambered up a screestrewn slope to see if he could catch a glimpse of those they had heard talking. When he returned, his face was grim. 'Well,' said Flint, 'what's the bad news, how many men out there?'

'I only saw the two.'

'Two? Hell's afire, man, I should say we can take on two men with a chance o' coming out atop of them.'

'It ain't that,' said Red Halliday slowly, 'one of 'em is that fellow as rode down on us yesterday. Him that fired at us, you recall?'

'Sure. You think he's after us? Law, maybe?'

'No, I recognize him now. I'd take oath that he was that big fellow that we paid to lend us a hand in Perseverance.'

'You certain sure?'

'I reckon so. It's him all right.'

Jake Flint was at first inclined to make light of the matter, saying, 'Well, he was a slow one. I doubt we've much to fear from him.'

'Why, you chucklehead, don't you see? He must have been following us all the way through the territories from

176

Kansas. You forgot that he saw us kill that farmer? That's a hanging matter, if ever I knew one.'

Flint was silent for a spell, as he mulled this over. Then he said, 'Best we take him out then, 'fore he takes it into his head to give information against us.'

Red Halliday shook his head. 'He's not thinking of that. My guess is he means to settle with us by his own self. Why else would he follow us all this time?'

'We best get after him then.'

So it was that without being at all aware of the fact, Chuck Mellors and Hector Grant changed at that moment from hunters to quarry.

★   ★   ★

After they set off that morning, Mellors and Grant found that they had been almost at the very top of the low range of mountains which they had been traversing the previous night. Cresting a low slope brought them onto a narrow plateau and crossing this led them to a sweeping vista of the plain below. In the distance could be seen a little town which, shining in the dawn air, looked like some fairy city. Grant said, 'Ah, distance lends enchantment to the view, as Mr Wordsworth said.'

'Mister who?'

'Wordsworth. William Wordsworth. He was a poet of whom my father was immensely fond.'

'That a fact?' asked Chuck Mellors, in a tone which suggested that he hadn't much use for poets at this present moment. 'More to the point, I thought you was some wonderful tracker. Yesterday you told me, if I recollect correctly, that if those boys don't actually fly, they couldn't escape your notice. Which way've they gone?'

Grant looked irritated to be badgered in this way and replied, 'You ever tried to track horses across bare rock like this? It's the very devil, I tell you. Don't trouble me now and I'll reason it out.'

The two men sat for a space, until at length, Hector Grant gave it as his opinion that the men for whom they were searching would most likely either already be in or, at the very least, be heading towards the town that could be seen shimmering on the horizon.

'You figure that out from the marks on these rocks?' enquired Mellors.

'Not precisely. They ain't up here and yet they came this way. Stands to reason that like us, they're apt to be getting hungry and that looks like the only place for miles where a body would have any chance of getting vittles.'

'Why, I could've told you the self-same thing,' said Mellors in disgust, 'without makin' myself out a red-hot scout or tracker!' He spurred on the mare and began threading his way through the boulders and scree towards the plain beneath them.

* * *

Neither Red Halliday nor his cousin had felt it needful to say out loud that they planned to commit murder. When

179

Flint had said earlier that they had best get after the man who was the only witness to the robbery and murder which they had undertaken in Perseverance, it had hardly been necessary for either of them to announce that the aim would be to silence that fellow for good and all. That the man was accompanied by somebody meant two killings rather than one but that was little to two such abandoned characters as that.

As they watched Mellors and Grant walking their mounts carefully down the rocky slopes, Jake Flint remarked to his cousin, 'There's no percentage in taking them on that level ground down there. They'd see us coming a mile off. Looks to me like they're heading east, to that little burg way over yon.'

'Happen so. Let's give 'em a good, long head start. You're right, they're sure to stop off in that town.'

So it was that these two sets of men, both set on killing each other, laid their plans for visiting the settlement of Hilton's Crossing.

Something like thirty years earlier, a Texan officer called James Hilton had forced his way through a vastly superior body of Mexican troops under the command of Santa Anna and then proceeded to decimate them in a brilliant cavalry charge on their flank. After the Mexicans had been routed, a little outpost had been set up on the spot, which became known as Hilton's Crossing, on account of that being the very place that James Hilton had crossed through Santa Anna's lines. Since Hilton had prevented the northward penetration of a sizeable force of Mexican soldiers which threatened American territory, it was felt right to commemorate his name in some way.

Over the years, what was once no more than a half-dozen soldiers manning a tiny outpost had grown to a town containing a little over 500 souls. Being positioned, as they were, on the very border between the Indian Territory and Texas, the folk of Hilton's Crossing were ideally placed to trade in whatever the Indians wished to buy. There were a number of foolish laws relating to the sale of hard liquor, powder and shot, firearms and the like to the Indians belonging to the so-called 'Five Civilized Tribes' but these were honoured in many parts of the country, more in the breach than the observance. In Hilton's Crossing, such laws were flagrantly disregarded in their entirety and whatever the Red Man wanted, he was able to obtain for a price.

As so often happens, the widespread ignoring of some laws turned in time to a contempt for the law in general. By the time that Chuck Mellors and Hector Grant reached Hilton's Crossing in the summer of 1871, the town was practically a law unto itself. Its position on the border helped of course, because neither the authorities in Texas nor the men of the Indian Bureau felt any great enthusiasm for dealing with such a pest-hole, both hoping that somebody else would eventually take action. In short, there was no kind of law enforcement in Hilton's Crossing, not even something as rudimentary as a vigilance committee and, as scripture has it, every man did that which was right in his own eyes.

* * *

It took Hector Grant no time at all to size up the town. Within minutes of riding in and walking their mounts down the main and only street of the town, he desired his companion to halt and said in a low voice, 'You know what sort of place this is, I'm guessing?'

'Somewhere that the odd shooting or killing ain't going to be too closely looked into, is what I reckon. Been in such little towns before.'

The two men watched an Indian walk past. This man was openly carrying a shining new army carbine which somebody had probably just sold him. Across the street, a group of swarthy-looking types, perhaps Comancheros, were sitting on the boardwalk. These men stared suspiciously at the two riders who had stopped near them, as though seeing a hostile act in anybody just remaining motionless in their vicinity. Grant sensed this and started his horse moving forward.

Chuck Mellors said, 'Well, I doubt anybody'll mind us bushwhacking those boys we're after, but on the other side, if they kill us first, then I can't see anybody worrying 'bout that neither.'

'You surely have a way with words,' replied Grant sourly, 'but I'd say you summed up the case nicely. To our advantage is that those dogs don't know we're coming after them.'

★   ★   ★

'Those dogs' were, as Hector Grant was speaking, three miles from Hilton's Crossing. They had not begun to ride down from the mountains until the men they were following were fairly on their way and unlikely to notice a couple of men three or four miles behind them. Before riding forward further, Red Halliday reined in and contemplated the scene before him for a little while, before remarking, 'I mind as I've been here before, you know.'

'Yeah? What is that town?'

'It's called something Crossing. Can't bring to mind right now.'

'What's it like there?' asked Flint. 'They got a sheriff or some other law?'

'No, last I was there, two, maybe three years back, there was nothing of the kind. It's wild land hereabouts. Folk tend to their own affairs and don't enquire overmuch about shootings, long as it's not their own kin that is. I saw two men shot there. Killed dead and nobody took a damned bit of notice. It's just perfect for us.'

'So what say? We ride in, deal with that big oaf that saw us steal those bonds and then carry on south?'

Red Halliday rubbed his chin meditatively. 'Yeah, I think you got it figured.

We don't want to linger here too long, just in case the Katy starts getting antsy about that train we stopped. We'll kill that fellow and then hightail it into Texas. Sooner we's across the Rio, safer I'll feel.'

'Well, what're we jawin' here for then?' asked Jake Flint and dug his spurs into the flanks of his horse. The two men set off at a canter towards Hilton's Crossing.

10

Chuck Mellors had not the faintest idea how they were to find the men he so urgently wished to tackle. Grant seemed a little uneasy, which was strange in a man who had struck him hitherto as being confident to the point of brashness. Mellors said, 'Something bothering you? You strike me as a mite edgy.'

'It don't signify.' He paused for a moment and then added, 'Thing is, this is not a town where it would be healthy for anybody to take somebody as being a bounty man, if you take my meaning. It might make folks a bit hostile.'

Chuck Mellors laughed and said, 'Cap fits, then wear it. I guess anybody has you pegged for a man of that brand ain't going to be too far wide of the mark.'

'Well then, and what's it to you?'

'Nothing at all. Only don't 'spect me

to stand friend to you if some villain here takes agin you and there's trouble. First off is where I don't care for bounty hunters myself and second, I got my own fish to fry.'

'Damned fine partner you're turning out to be!' growled Hector Grant, irritated but not at all surprised. 'Come on, let's go into the barrooms round here and see if we can't run those boys to earth.'

Mellors and Grant tethered their mounts to the hitching rail outside the nearest saloon, which was called The Luck of the Draw. Inside, the bar was all but deserted; it was not yet nine in the morning. The owner was polishing the tables and there were only a couple of men standing at the bar, nursing small glasses of ale. Mellors went up to the man who was wiping down the tables and said, 'Me and my friend are looking for a fellow with bright red, carroty hair. Bring anybody to mind?'

'Couldn't say,' said the man, without looking up, 'I don't notice men's appearance all that much.' Chuck Mellors interpreted this, quite correctly, as a snub and indication that questions like that weren't welcomed in the place.

The story was much the same with the other two bars they tried. This was definitely the sort of town where men asking searching questions and trying to track somebody down were not welcomed with open arms. After they had received their final rebuff, the two men left the saloon and stood outside in the morning sunshine.

'If you really are a bounty hunter,' remarked Mellors, 'then I hope you got some more ideas on finding those two fellows. Can't say as I'm overly impressed so far and that's a fact.'

★   ★   ★

They say that old sins cast long shadows and the truth of this aphorism was amply demonstrated to Red Halliday and his cousin when they rode into Hilton's Crossing that morning, just as

Chuck Mellors and Hector Grant had made their third fruitless visit to the local saloons.

When he had last been in this town, two years after the War Between the States had ended in 1865, Red Halliday had been engaged in a scheme to cheat some very rough customers out of their money. He had sold a consignment of weapons, modern rifles which had been surrendered by the Confederate Army and acquired dirt cheap from a disaffected sergeant working in an arsenal. What Halliday had known, but the men to whom he was selling them did not, was that these had all been seized by the Union forces as part of the surrender terms and then rendered inoperable by the simple expedient of opening the breach and breaking off the firing pins from the bolts.

The fellows to whom Red Halliday had sold all this useless weaponry had traded it across the Rio Grande to rebels there who were organizing the insurrection which would ultimately overthrow

the Emperor Maximillian. The Comancheros who bought the rifles from Halliday
had not only been cheated out of a
considerable sum of money but later
had their very lives put in hazard when
the Mexican revolutionists to whom they
sold them found that the guns were
utterly useless. These men, not unnatu-
rally, assumed that the Comancheros
had deliberately set out to cheat them
and the traders had nearly paid with
their lives for this misunderstanding. When
eventually they had made it back alive
across the Rio, the men had sworn a
solemn oath that should they ever catch
sight again of that red-headed bastard
who had almost cost them their lives,
there would be a bloody reckoning.

He had over the years been so much
in the habit of cheating others and,
where the opportunity presented itself,
stealing from them, that Red Halliday
had more or less forgotten the precise
details of the stunt which he had pulled
when last he was in Hilton's Crossing.
At the back of his mind was the idea

that he had steered clear of this burg for a few years, but the details were vague. Anyway, he was not planning on staying long now and most likely those whom he had crossed when last he visited would be dead by now.

As Halliday and his cousin trotted into town, a small group of loafers sprawled on the boardwalk eyed them incuriously until one of them caught sight of the flaming red locks under one of the riders' hat. He looked harder at the man's face and then nudged his neighbour and jerked his head in the direction in which he had been staring. The other man started visibly and then a cruel smile appeared on his lips. He said to his *compadre*, 'You think it is he, without a doubt?'

'It is he.'

The two of them got to their feet and, telling the other men that they had some important business that they had just recollected, went off at a brisk pace in pursuit of Red Halliday and Jake Flint.

If the matter at hand had not been so deadly serious, then there would have been something irresistibly comic about the situation in Hilton's Crossing that morning; three pairs of men, all determined to kill each other and none of them realizing the actual state of affairs. It was like something from a comic opera. On the one hand, Chuck Mellors and Hector Grant thought that they were hunting down two men, who were actually hunting for them and aiming to shoot them. Unbeknown to them though, two other men were fixing to kill one of these hunters in turn. It was perhaps inevitable that blood would flow that day.

Red Halliday said, 'Wait up now, I see those men from the train. Over yonder, standing by the horses, there.'

'By God, you're right,' replied Flint. 'You want to just kill them now and then dig up? We got no provisions, you know. Could do with 'quiring some before we leave here.'

'Provisions be damned to you, that

man can hang us by just opening his mouth too wide.'

'Well, you got a point there, I guess. Let's do it!'

It was at this point that a ball went droning past Halliday's head and since he was watching the two men from the train, he knew at once that he and his cousin were caught between two enemies; one forward and the other behind. He wasted little thought on this circumstance, beyond registering it in his mind. Red Halliday was essentially a man of action, rather than a deep thinker. That being so, he spurred on his mount and then rode around in a tight circle until he was facing the direction from which he had been coming. As he did so, he contrived to draw his pistol, cocking it with his thumb as he did so.

It took no great effort to see who had just taken a shot at Halliday, because two men were standing in the road, with guns in their hands. They commenced firing again at Halliday, who returned fire at once, hitting one of the men in the face with a fantastically lucky shot. Jake Flint was also in the game now and the remaining man dived for cover. Other people who had been passing in the street were now running about like headless chickens, exceedingly anxious not to be caught in the crossfire from the gun battle which had just erupted.

Hector Grant had not drawn his pistol when the first shot was fired, a little down the street from himself and Mellors. Instead, because they were standing right by his mount, he reached over and pulled a carbine from where it nestled in its scabbard at the front of the saddle. He worked the handle, cocking the piece and putting a cartridge in the chamber, them moved around the horses, being sure to keep them between him and the part of that street where the sound of the shot had come from. Chuck Mellors, being a simpler soul, had simply pulled his beat-up old Navy Colt from the worn holster at his hip and begun scanning the street behind him. It didn't take him long to pick out the two riders

195

who were seemingly under attack and it came as no surprise to him that it was the men he had been involved with briefly in Perseverance. Since it appeared to be open season, he too fired at the man with the red hair, his ball missing Halliday and going on to shatter an upstairs window in the doctor's surgery above one of the stores.

Both Halliday and Flint realized immediately that two sets of men were now trying to kill them. While Halliday exchanged shots with the Comanchero, who was crouching behind a bunch of goods set out in front of a general store, Jake Flint turned his attentions to those up ahead. He tried to avoid killing anybody's horse, because he had seen men driven into a killing rage by such carelessness and he had not the least desire to draw anybody else into the battle being waged against him and his cousin. This was difficult, because somebody was snapping off shots with a rifle, using the horses as cover. Flint kept his horse jittering sideways, which

196

had the effect of making him a more tricky target, but also spoiled his own aim.

While Grant kept one of the riders busy, Chuck Mellors simply strolled along the boardwalk, his pistol held behind his back so that it could not be seen. Then, when he was level with one of the men whom he recognized as having recruited him in the robbery of the farmer, Mellors simply brought his gun out and shot the fellow in the back of the head. As he did so, Red Halliday finally managed to take the second Comanchero, who had left the cover of the pots, pans, crates and boxes stacked outside the store and essayed a crouching run to a doorway. Halliday's ball took him in the chest and the fellow cartwheeled through the dirt and then lay still.

As soon as he was sure that there was no more fire likely to come from that part of the street, Halliday turned around and saw at once that his cousin Jake had been either mortally wounded or killed. Flint had tumbled from his horse and was now lying in the roadway, tangled into an awkward heap. For all that they bickered, Red Halliday was genuinely fond of his cousin and now desired only to put an end to whoever had shot Jake. Mellors sprinted forward, hoping to take the rider by surprise, but Halliday was not to be caught so lightly. He fired once at the man charging towards him, but when he fired a second time, the hammer clicked uselessly and he knew that he had used up both pistols, with no present chance of reloading. This was pretty much the last thought of Halliday's life, because no sooner had the realization struck him than Hector Grant had stepped clear of the horses behind which he had been sheltering and, kneeling down to improve his aim, had fired twice at Halliday. Both balls found lodging places, one in the chest and the other in the stomach.

For a fraction of a second, Red Halliday could not quite take in what had chanced. He had never yet been bested in a gunfight. Then he felt his senses failing and he slumped forward, his eyes closing for the last time.

After a shootout of this sort, there is generally a silence, as those who have had no part in it weigh up the odds and try to work out whether or not it is safe to step back into the open. Depending on circumstances, this pause before things return to anything like normal takes upwards of thirty seconds or a few minutes. In Hilton's Crossing, they were perhaps more familiar with episodes of sanguinary violence than the average town, so the citizens tended to recover their equanimity somewhat more rapidly. The echoes of the shooting had scarcely had time to die down before some of those who had been cowering below the windows of the stores lining the street had emerged and were drifting over to see who had been killed.

Mellors did not waste any time in getting down to what he saw as the real purpose of his mission in the town, namely, getting hold of the bearer-bonds, which had been the reason that he had become embroiled in this business in the first place. He marched straight over to where Red Halliday was sitting dead in the saddle of his horse and began searching first the saddle bag and then the dead man's pockets. Those watching began to suspect that the whole aim of the shooting had been no more than a robbery.

When he had drawn a blank with the red-headed man's person and belongings, Mellors went over to where the other body lay and was enormously surprised to discover that Jake Flint was still in the land of the living. True, he was breathing rapidly and shallowly, as though on his last legs, but he was still conscious. The shot which Chuck Mellors had fired had taken a chunk of Flint's skull off at the back and it was not hard to see that he wouldn't recover from the wound, but for now at least, his eyes were open and although he couldn't move, he was looking around him fearfully.

Mellors squatted down next to the dying man and said, 'Well, I'm sorry for you, fellow, but you chose this road for yourself.'

'I can't feel my legs,' said Flint in a thin and reedy voice, 'am I hurt bad?'

'Bad enough. Don't try and move. You a Christian? I could say a prayer if you like.'

'Hell, no. It's late in the day for that. Never thought I'd see you again.'

Chuck Mellors found this situation more awkward and embarrassing than anything else. Here he was, chatting normally to a man he had shot and who was about to die shortly. He swallowed and said in as natural a tone as he could manage, 'Can I get you a drink of water or aught?'

'No, I'm tired. Think I'm goin' to sleep now.'

Whereupon the man that lay in the road closed his eyes, took a couple of gulping breaths, yawned and suddenly went into a seizure, twitching and gulping until his body went floppy and he stopped breathing. Somebody standing nearby said, 'Lord have mercy on his soul.'

'Amen,' said Mellors and then reflected that this was a strange way to carry on, seeing as it had been he himself who had killed the fellow. Cold-hearted as it might have looked to those standing nearby, he reached inside the dead man's jacket and found that there was a stiff bundle of documents in a buttoned pocket. Drawing these out, they proved to be the bonds for which he had been looking. He tucked them into his own pocket and then stood up.

While all this had been going on, Hector Grant had been dealing with Halliday, dragging him off his horse and then slinging the corpse unceremoniously over the saddle. Having done this, Grant went over to his own horse and extracted a piece of rawhide from the bag and came back to his trophy. He lashed the dead man's wrists and ankles together under the belly of the horse and then joined Mellors, saying, 'You got what you wanted?'

Nobody troubled either Mellors or Grant, but it was fairly apparent that most of those in the vicinity did not care for what must have looked like the looting of bodies. The fact that Hector Grant was now evidently intent on making off with the dead men showed beyond all doubt that here were bounty killers at work, a breed for whom nobody in Hilton's Crossing had any affection at all. Mellors said quietly to Grant, 'You best make haste. I'm ready to move out and if you don't finish up here soon, I'm leaving without you. Can't you see that folk hereabouts don't care for these carryings on?'

Grant shrugged and said, 'I need some food, 'fore I'm leaving this town, I'll tell you that for nothing! You're too sensitive.'

Now that the subject had been mentioned, it struck Chuck Mellors forcibly that he too was ravenously hungry. There looked to be no sign of any aggressive action against either him or Grant; the disapproval was manifested only in the disgusted expressions on the men standing nearby as they watched Grant heave

Jake Flint over the saddle of the dead man's horse, like he might have been a sack of potatoes. The unfavourable impression created by this callous disdain for a recently deceased human person was in no way lessened by the fact that as the body was dumped over the saddle, part of the skull at the back of the head came loose and some of Flint's brain matter dropped into the roadway. There were murmurs when this happened and Mellors said to the other man, 'I'll be down the road aways in that eating house we passed when first we entered town. You want to meet me there, that's fine. Else we can go our own separate ways from hereon in, if that'd suit you better.'

'I'll be with you in just a few minutes,' replied Grant, 'I need to get this all fixed up.' He spoke about the human cargo which he was securing with as little emotion as if they had been a couple of butchered shoats. Even for Chuck Mellors, who was a fairly unimaginative and tough individual, this was all a little much. As he led his horse down the street, he reflected that this must be the effect that being a bounty man had upon one. It led to a coarsening of sensibilities and a general disregard for death. True, he himself had killed one of those men, but he still recognized the man he had shot as a fellow being, deserving of some decency and respect. Hector Grant appeared to have no such feelings.

Nobody seemed to be too concerned about the two Comancheros who had been killed and their bodies were lying right where they had been shot. Although he and Grant had had no hand in those deaths, it did occur to Mellors that if the men had any friends hereabouts, then they might find some blame attaching to themselves for what had happened. This was another good reason to clear out of this town as swiftly as might be.

The owner of the eating house showed little curiosity about the crash of gunfire which had just disturbed the morning. He had heard it, but since it was a few yards from his establishment, he saw no reason to concern himself. He provided Mellors with some bread, cheese and onions, which, since he had not begun to cook yet that day, was pretty much all that was immediately available. Shortly after Mellors began to eat, Hector Grant appeared. Through the window, the horses laden with the corpses of their late owners could be seen at the hitching rail. When Grant had also acquired some bread and cheese, he came over and sat opposite Chuck Mellors, who observed quietly, 'You might as well have set up a poster outside, saying 'Bounty Killer at work'.'

'I doubt they're kin to anybody here. Those other fellows seemed dead set on killing 'em as well, you know.'

'Which way are you heading now?' asked Mellors. 'I ask, because I'm bound for Kansas. I have business that way.'

'Something to do with those bonds you took from that fellow's coat pocket?'

'Never you trouble yourself about my affairs,' said Mellors in a voice which was intended to cut short any further debate. 'It's enough that I am going north. What about you?'

'I think I'll travel along of you, if that's agreeable?'

Mellors gave an ungracious shrug. He had no time at all for men who lived by the death of others and would, truth to tell, have sooner travelled alone. He thought that he would find an excuse to do so once they left, because of course the bounty killer and his troop of horses would make slow going. There'd be no question of moving along at anything faster than a trot. All he needed was to say that he wanted to make a faster pace and he would have the perfect excuse just to canter off and leave this disagreeable fellow to his own devices. Lord knows, Mellors had no special desire anyway to ride alongside a couple of corpses!

After he had finished eating and had a couple of cups of good, strong coffee inside him, Chuck Mellors intimated that he was about to leave. A more sensitive man than Hector Grant might have taken this as a hint, but Grant was not at all like that. He merely exclaimed, 'Wait up, while I finish my coffee and we'll be on our way. Don't be in such a hurry, man!'

Once the two of them were clear of the town and fairly on their way, heading into the territories, Mellors decided that he would bide his time and ride along with Grant until the afternoon. Although he owed him nothing, it sat ill with Chuck Mellors to just race off and leave the other man to make his solitary way wherever he was going. It was by this time about half past ten, which meant that Mellors only needed to put up with the others' company for a few more hours. Feeling slightly guilty about planning to abandon the other, although the Lord only knew why he should feel so, Mellors thought to make a little conversation. He accordingly asked, 'What's this work that you hope to do with the Katy, then?'

Grant shot him a sideways glance, almost, thought Mellors, a cunning look. 'Oh, the Katy's always on the lookout for fellows like me, you know. Boys who can keep folk safe.'

He knew it was ill-natured of him, but Chuck Mellors could not forebear to chuckle at that point and say, 'What, safe like that lady that was coming south on the Katy Flyer? Or the fireman, for the matter of that?'

This time the look that Grant gave him had more to it than merely dislike; it was one of pure hatred. Although Mellors's remarks had been meant only as a little light-hearted joshing, it was pretty obvious that they had struck home deeply. Grant said, 'You think you're pretty damned smart, don't you?'

'Not specially so,' replied Mellors imperturbably. 'Just making conversation. Don't take on so.'

There was a long silence, which was at last broken by Grant saying, 'You never did tell me what the story was about you, those men and the bearer-bonds.'

'Hey, that's right. I never did.'

'Well?' said Hector Grant, his voice taut with barely suppressed anger. 'What's the story?'

'None o' your affair.'

'You don't think so?'

'I know so,' said Mellors and then, tiring of the whole thing, he added, 'Cards on the table. I don't care for you none, any more'n you seem to for me. Never had any use for bounty hunters at the best o' times and you are one poisonous member of the species. That being so, maybe it's best if we part company now. I'll be on my way.'

'No, you don't,' said Hector Grant in a low, savage voice. 'You just set right there and don't move your hand anywhere near to that piece of yours.'

When Chuck Mellors turned to face his travelling companion, it was to find that Grant was drawing down on him with his pistol and judging from the look on his face, he was in no mood to parlay.

11

There could be not the slightest doubt that this was a tricky and uncertain situation. Temporizing, and wondering how matters would pan out, Mellors said in a reasonable tone, 'Mind telling me what this is about?'

'You're suspicioned for murder and robbery is what it's about. As if you didn't know.'

There was an awkward pause, while Mellors worked out what he was going to do next. One thing was certain, he repented of that little crack about the safety of those passengers on the Katy Flyer. That really seemed to have riled up the bounty man. Hector Grant said, 'You'll tell me you're as innocent as a new-born babe, is that the way of it?'

'What's your aim?'

'My aim? To take you back to Kansas with these boys. I tell you now, I'd as soon take you back dead as I would alive. I always found dead men safer and easier to transport, to speak bluntly. But you do just as I bid you and I might consent to your staying alive.'

Chuck Mellors said with a dejected air, 'Looks to me like you hold all the cards here. What would you have me do?'

'That's the sensible dodge. I'll tell you what I require of you. You take out that pistol of yours and hand it to me, hilt first. But slow as you like, or by God I'll shoot you down like a dog. I've already taken first pull and you make any sudden movement and we'll not be able to put matters right in this world, you hear what I'm saying?'

'Sure. I ain't what you'd call a fast mover. Look, I'm reaching for it, real slow, just like you said.'

It would have been plain to the meanest intelligence that Hector Grant was not bluffing and would most likely be only too glad to gun down the man reaching for his pistol. Mellors sensed that his very life hung by a thread, but even at this moment he was more concerned about the fact that Grant struck him as the sort of greedy and ruthless man who would probably steal the bonds for himself and deprive Mellors of the chance to make amends to that poor widow and her child.

Very carefully, so as not to give the man drawing on him any excuse to fire, Mellors hooked his index finger through the trigger guard of his pistol and slowly lifted it clear of the holster. It hung there, upside down and with the hilt pointing towards Grant. He said, 'Well, you want me to throw it clear?'

'And have it go off as it hits the ground? No, I'm going to walk my horse forward and take it from you. You just sit there, still as a stock, hear me?'

Mellors's face wore a dejected, hangdog look as he nodded his assent. The bounty hunter moved forward slowly and then, when his horse was only a couple of feet away, he reached out his hand to take the weapon being proffered to him. Chuck Mellors sat as immobile as a statue, his hand stretched out in front of him, offering the weapon to be taken. The Navy Colt hung from his forefinger and all that was needed was for Grant to reach out and take it. As he did so, something immensely surprising, at least to him, occurred.

Although the pistol hung upside down and with the hilt facing Hector Grant, it needed only the merest flick of the wrist to turn it round and bring the gun nestling snugly in Mellors's grasp. Grant had shifted the pistol in his right hand as he stretched out his left, so that it was no longer pointing straight at the man he was disarming; he was that assured that Chuck Mellors was wholly within his power. It was a fatal mistake for one usually so careful, because as soon as that little twist had brought his gun comfortably into his hand, Mellors cocked and fired in one smooth movement. At that range, he could scarcely have missed and the ball ploughed straight through the centre of Grant's chest, shattering his breastbone and shredding his heart.

The physical shock of the assault to his vital organs caused Hector Grant's whole body to contort and all his muscles to contract convulsively. This in turn made his hand twitch, which fired his pistol; sending a ball straight into the neck of Mellors's horse, which then bucked in fear and pain, throwing her rider.

When he picked himself up, Chuck Mellors saw at once that he was now the only person alive in the vicinity. His mare was whinnying in distress and blood was pumping from a jagged tear through her throat.

'All right, girl,' he said softly and then, after picking up the pistol which had fallen from his hand when he had taken a tumble, he went over and began comforting the terrified creature. There was no point in prolonging her agony so he raised the gun and put a single shot cleanly through the horse's head.

She fell at once, as though pole-axed.

There were now three living horses standing around the roadway, each of them bearing a corpse, as well as the dead mare. This was such a singular circumstance that Mellors found it a little disconcerting. He knew that he would have to cut sticks as soon as could be, for it would invite lengthy explanations, were anybody to come upon this scene. Nevertheless, some sense of what was fitting and right impelled him to say a few words over the body of the man he had just killed. He was not a religious man so he limited his remarks to the practicalities of what had just happened.

'I'm sorry as I killed you,' said Mellors, 'but you were going to kill me all along anyway at some stage and it was no more than you deserved, really. I'd have thought a man in your trade might have known about the border roll or what some call the 'road agent's spin'. What I did with my gun, I mean, when I made out I was going to let you have it. Anyways, it's an old enough trick.

'Still, there it is. You died and I didn't. Can't say as I'm sorry. You lived your life as seemed good to you and now you died in the same way. There it is.'

After completing this little speech, Mellors wondered if he should perhaps say 'amen', but then that would be crazy, because he wasn't even sure if any of these three dead men were likely to be feasting with the Lord in paradise right now. A more practical consideration was which of the horses he should take to replace his own. After examining them all, he thought that Hector Grant's was in better shape than the other two, which were scrawny and underfed creatures.

After transferring his own saddle to Grant's horse, Chuck Mellors did something which he felt in some obscure way to be unethical and wrong. Still, the events of the last week or so had had the effect of blunting his own finer feelings to some extent. When he had been invited back at Seward's Folly to join in the looting of a dead body, he had been horrified. Since then, though, he had searched the corpse of that red-haired rascal without giving it a second thought. So it was that he now set about searching the three bodies, which were his only present companions, for anything worth taking. After all, he reasoned, if he left the bodies here then the next person to pass along the road would most likely steal anything he didn't himself take. The bundle of wanted bills and newspaper cuttings in Hector Grant's possession occasioned him no surprise, but finding that Grant had $200 tucked away was a pleasant discovery. The other two men yielded just under $100 between the two of them. Still, Mellors now had enough to tide him over for a good long while and some more after overcoming his reservations about looting the corpses.

By a great mercy, nobody else had

come down the road while all these transactions had been taking place, which was a relief to the man who had been delving into the jackets and bags of the dead men. After he had finished, Mellors took down the bodies and laid them by the side of the road. Then he untacked the two horses that he would not be using and turned them loose. The gear, he piled alongside the corpses, free to all takers. Then he set off north, towards Kansas.

It is a satisfying and comforting feeling, knowing that you have done your duty, in as much as it has been possible. The only slight, niggling problem which remained was how to get those blessed bearer-bonds to the widow of the slain farmer. Chuck Mellors had a sneaking feeling at the back of his mind that he would be most ill-advised to return to Perseverance at all, let alone to go back to the town and start enquiring about the whereabouts of Richard Carstairs's widow and relict. No, he would have to find another way. The idea, when it came to him, seemed like pure genius. This was particularly so because he was not a man for planning and stratagems in general and such thinking did not come easily to him.

For a souvenir of this episode, Mellors had taken from the bounty hunter's pack the newspaper piece concerning the robbery in which he had been an unwilling participant. Grant had saved the entire page and at the bottom was printed the name and address of the publisher, which was evidently to be found in the town of Walker's Landing. It was accordingly to that location that Chuck Mellors directed himself. It took the better part of four days to cross the Indian Nations and once he was in Kansas, it was another day's ride to Walker's Crossing, where, according to the page in Hector Grant's pack, *The South Kansas Plain Dealer, incorporating the Walker's Landing Agricultural Gazette and Intelligencer* had its offices and was printed.

Artifice did not come easily to Chuck Mellors so he thought that the more quickly this enterprise was dealt with, the better it would be. Walker's Landing was a bustling little town and some thought that it would soon become the County Seat. The newspaper's premises were all but next door to the sheriff's office, which occasioned Mellors some little unease when first he observed the proximity of the two buildings. Mind, he would be in and out in just a minute at most and the scope for trouble was strictly limited.

After leaving his, or more accurately, Hector Grant's, horse at the hitching rail outside the newspaper offices, Mellors opened the door and entered the place. The front office at first appeared to be deserted, but when the door closed with a sudden and unexpected crash, a little old man stood up from where he had been crouched behind the counter looking at some proofs.

'Yes?' he said querulously. 'What's all the noise about? What do you want?'

'It's kind of delicate,' said Chuck Mellors. 'Me and some others, we read about that poor woman, that Mrs Carstairs, whose husband was killed. We hoped to do something to help her.'

'Yes, terrible, terrible. What of it then?'

'If I give you something of benefit to her, would you be able to forward it?'

'Yes, yes. Of course we will, only too happy to help in any way.' The proprietor of the South Kansas Plain Dealer was not a man to pass up the opportunity for a little free publicity and could already see how this would make another human interest feature in the next edition of the paper. 'Let's have this then. What is it, cash money or what?'

Chuck Mellors took the leather satchel from his shoulder. He had dumped and burned all the wanted bills and other paperwork it had once contained and placed in there only the bearer-bonds, which had been at the centre of all the trouble. He said, 'Listen, I hope that I can trust you. If I find later that the contents of this bag didn't reach Mrs Carstairs, why, there'd be an awful stink.'

The old man flushed crimson and said stiffly, 'You need have not the slightest apprehension on that score, young fellow.'

'I trust you,' said Mellors and, after handing the bag to the old man, turned to leave.

'Hold up, what name was it?'

'That's of no account. So long.'

Although no great student of human nature, it had struck Chuck Mellors that receiving the stolen bonds in this way would probably make the editor of that newspaper's day. The ceremonious handing over of them to the widow Carstairs would perhaps be the main item on the front page of the next edition of *The South Kansas Plain Dealer*, and that old fellow would most likely dine out on the story of how a stranger walked into his office and just handed over the proceeds of the robbery in that casual way.

It made sense, though, not to linger in the vicinity of the newspaper office, just on the remote off chance that the man he had handed that satchel to would come running out into the street and start shouting about the contents. It would be the hell of a thing, having got so far, to end up being arrested for that robbery at this late stage.

It was Chuck Mellors's considered opinion that the further he was from Walker's Landing and Perseverance, then the better it was apt to be for him. As he headed to the outskirts of town and the road leading west, he ran over in his mind the situation in which he currently found himself. On the debit side, he was nominally wanted for robbery with violence and murder. It would be prudent not to revisit the town where that unfortunate misunderstanding had arisen but other than that, he couldn't see that the affair was likely to follow him wherever he went. Lord knows there were enough such crimes committed and he surely wasn't the only big man in south Kansas.

Looking at the credit side of the balance sheet gave a more rosy view of things. Mellors now had in total something in the region of $340 in cash money. Living frugally, at the rate of, say twenty-five dollars a week, this sum would take care of his needs for three months or more. This was a damned sight better than the position in which he had been placed before he'd been drawn into that robbery.

As he reached the last few houses on the edge of Walker's Landing, Chuck Mellors saw that somebody had erected a rough finger post, which pointed in the direction in which he was riding. It informed him that the town of Parsons was thirty-five miles away. This caused the young man to frown a little and wonder why that name sounded familiar. Of course, it was because the Katy ran through the town. Then Mellors began ravelling thread and recalled the warnings that Jim Seward had given him and also the circumstance of that skunk Grant being on the train and angling for a job with the railroad. Well, he, Chuck Mellors, was mighty handy with a gun himself, if it came to it. Maybe he could do worse than drift over to Parsons and see if the Katy might want somebody like him working for them to guard their trains. His late exploit in foiling the robbery of the Katy Flyer might be a recommendation, perhaps.

Mellors felt a sudden and unexpected surge of optimism and he began whistling a merry little tune. Then he spurred on the horse and began trotting down the road towards Parsons.